*for Valeria,
this book 7 wounds
& light.
With affection
Maria
2019*

The
Annunciation

By María Negroni

Translated by Michelle Gil-Montero

Action Books
Notre Dame, Indiana 2019

Action Books

Joyelle McSweeney and Johannes Göransson, Editors
Anne Malin Ringwalt, 2017-2019 Editorial Assistant
Natasha Ali, Maxime Berclaz and Sebastian Bostwick, 2018-2020 Editorial Assistants
Andrew Shuta, Book Design
Don Mee Choi and Daniel Borzutzky, Advisory Board

The Annunciation
@2019, María Negroni and Michelle Gil-Montero
@2007, Emicé Editores S.A./Seix Barral, Independencia 1668, C1100ABQ
Buenos Aires
@2006, María Negroni

First Edition

ISBN 978-0-900575-81-5

Library of Congress Control Number: 2018961486

Action Books is housed in the Creative Writing Program, Department of English,
College of Arts & Letters, University of Notre Dame. We can be reached at
356 O'Shaughnessy Hall, Notre Dame, IN, 46556.

actionbooks.org

The Annunciation

*To Humboldt, who maybe was or might have been,
and who is still alive in words that haven't been written.*

I write as if trying to save someone's life.
Probably my own.

Clarice Lispector

I.
Earthly Paradise

I don't know how to tell the story of a death, Humboldt. Least of all, a death like mine, which was life in the end.

It went something like this: you left, and I died, and one morning I woke up shouting, *I'm going to throw a party, I want to offer my night to the people, I won't blow it*, like Quasimodo, *prowling around the Cathedral of Evil*. So I called you *My Little Distant Sunshine* one last time and locked you in the closet. That night *my* Private Life came over. She just waltzed in, plopped on the couch, and demanded that I stop losing myself in order to find you. She sternly reminded me: "Rome exists." I didn't dare to object. Then, as soon as she was confident of her power over me, she boiled water for tea and asked me how long I'd believed in Pure Evil.

"Since I met Humboldt," I admitted.

"You're hopeless," she said, "always the extremist."

"Extremist? I thought I dropped out of the movement ages ago."

"Don't fool yourself," she answered.

All the power had gone to her head.

Actually I died and resurrected. I'd tell myself, "I've got a plan, I'll write a still life and put myself into it. If I look hard enough, I'll find a shadow. Shadows will be there for me, I shouldn't fear, I just need to remember that everything could end tomorrow, that everything will, in fact, end tomorrow, and then I won't need to wear my grief like an amulet, I won't have to keep Humboldt prisoner in the closet, safe from the terrible things that my imagination constantly (right now, for instance) dictates to me."

"You and your drastic decisions!" my Private Life remarked.

Once I ran away like a mourning heroine. I was wearing a little wool hat and high-heeled boots, and before I knew it, I was standing in the middle of the street with my keys in my hand and no clue where to go. *I shall be too late!*, it occurred to me, like Alice's White Rabbit, so I stopped the first passerby and asked: "Could you point me to the Office of Lost Ideals?" He looked shocked. There was something vaguely familiar about him. "That's all history," he replied and left me standing there holding my keys. I forget what happened next. Probably nothing. I started living in two cities at once. I got used to having two houses, two libraries, two bedside tables, two of everything, except your body, Humboldt, was in neither place, and no train or plane, no mode of transportation, could take me to you.

My Private Life said, "Here we go again. How many pages did you write today?"

"Look," I replied, "I'm planning to knuckle down. I'll write two pages a day, I promise."

Saying so, oddly enough, reassured me. I knew that I

was grieving, that I loved you so much that I couldn't eat, sleep, advance my career, go to the beach, buy an ice cream. What is *that* feeling called?

"Just look at yourself," my Private Life said. "You're a wreck. You've got to move on." She then proceeded to lecture me about toxic thinking, but honestly, I had no idea what she was talking about, when I tried to imagine the thoughts she was referring to, they seemed so beautiful: you and I lost, like orphaned children, in a derelict garden—isn't that gorgeous?

Right now, for example, your death circles the universe like you're embracing me at last, I feel so *terribly* protected. But no one would ever guess it, not even me. I only mention it because I want you to know why I'm not as sad as I should be. See? There's no shaking my faith in life's happiness. I'm uttering words that haven't been invented yet. (And I'm trembling, and your back is turned to me.) The words sound like apples. One bite, then another, and in the end, you're still hungry. Failure, Humboldt, is an uprooting, it only pretends to be an ending but really things have just begun and will go on forever, like a starry night, riddled with ghosts. That's how I died and resurrected. I died and kept fighting, until exhausted, and yours forever, I wiped you from my life.

Call it an *Internal Revolution*, G.I. Joe battling his own double. What was missing between us? (I forget.)

I need you to help me with something. I want you to report my Private Life. She won't stop harassing me. She shows up, rain or shine, one day in a new dress, another with blonde highlights, if you saw her, you'd call her a dirty bourgeois. One day she told me, "Go ahead and sulk for a hundred years if you like, torture yourself, look for the moral in the beating, but you

‹3›

have to admit, a haircut can work miracles—what, don't you like me?"

I turned my head, I couldn't fake it, you would have crucified me. You who built a fortress to protect us from phonies, posers, frauds.

"Can she even hear herself?" my Private Life soliloquized insidiously, "You'd think she wanted to die again!"

"No, I don't want to die," I said. "I want to live. I want to live my blindness to the fullest."

Do I sound crazy, Humboldt? Do these orphan words make any sense?

Now I'm in Rome. The house with green walls is far away. So far that it resembles an island buried in snow. I wonder whether I was happy there, with you or alone, for how long. I wish you'd appear, this instant, to clarify things. But nobody's here, apart from my Private Life and my grief. It's like someone opened a wound in me, and then another inside it, and another, then caged a swallow inside. Humboldt, I'm slandering you, there are no swallows in Rome, nothing could have been avoided, it's that simple, and so without complaint, I gathered my sails and set straight for the unwavering port, one, two, three, I told myself, what survives today will die tomorrow, why delay the beauty of the inevitable?

Everything, Humboldt, has a shadow, and death has the greatest shadow of all. I mean that time passes, no one seems to notice, and living is our only option. So that's what I did, like the newborn woman I was, I forced it, I stifled myself, and totally miserable, I stopped telling lies. (Beauty is a subtle lie.)

The miracle wasn't foreign to Rome.

For some reason, when you move there, you forget who

you used to be. It's incredible. With every step, you get farther away from yourself, like you've come from nothing.

This is resurrection.

To be given the gift of a second childhood.

At first I just stood in the middle of the street looking lost, absent, happy. The military had stopped haunting me. I'd even wander into toy stores to admire the little lead soldiers.

Sometimes I'd run into Emma. I'd see her strolling along the gilt edges of the city, a figure cloaked in humility, which is to say, a profound sense of inherent freedom. Those nights in Rome will never fade from my mind. Emma teasing me, "Alright, what can you say about this river, or this summer, or the sandmen you'll meet someday in a godforsaken desert?" Then she'd toss me a cigarette or a newspaper, and I'd catch a glimmer of something hidden, something that far, far exceeds, I know now, what we see.

That's enough for now, Humboldt. Who knows if we'll see each other again, or when. Goodbye. I'll leave you to that bright blank that is and was (and ever shall be) what we might have been together.

March 11, 1976, he's twenty-two.

He doesn't smoke. He can't play chess. He has no travel plans in his agenda, and no notes about the seven heavens of Islam or Censorius of Smyrna who once observed the Fixed Stars one octave from Earth.

According to the Secretariat of State Intelligence, who has been keeping him under surveillance, he is a subversive element, a seditious individual, a threat to patriotic interests. The police report states: Level of Education, High School; Military Rank, High; Attitude Toward Reality, Denial.

Would he have had kids? Maybe. But maybe not.

In any case, he never would have named them: Albano Jorge, Hermes José, Reynaldo Benito, Cesario Ángel, Jorge Rafael, Luciano Benjamín, Emilio Eduardo, Orlando Ramón, or Leopoldo Fortunato.

The chronology of his downfall can't be established with certainty.

He has no first name.

Just an alias:

Humboldt.

"Athanasius," the monk announced as he sat down beside me in the Piazza Farnese, "creator of the First World Museum, at your service."

I felt like I was reading a book that, out of nowhere, took a turn for the absurd.

"What was that?" I managed to ask.

"In 1646, I founded a museum that contains, or duplicates, the world."

"Oh."

My mind retraced his words as if contemplating a lunar eclipse. Two celestial bodies, equally arbitrary, crossing along a mechanism that I couldn't understand, just like I couldn't understand the girls in the Piazza Farnese, marching to the clatter of high heels, their hair swarmed by butterflies.

"You wouldn't happen to be the young lady who used to

visit the apartment on la calle Uruguay?"

The monk didn't wait for an answer. After motioning for me to follow him, he cut into a dark alley. He seemed a little purblind, permissive, like someone who has brushed with Death. In his eyes, a swallow took flight toward an invisible zenith.

"I've wanted to meet you for a long time," he said suddenly. "Here, take my card. If you're ever in the area, I'd like to give you a tour of my Museum."

The night towered over us. My question echoed like a shot.

"Did you know Emma?"

"Of course."

He paused briefly and gestured for me to sit beside him on a narrow stoop.

"You see," he said as I sat down, "I have friends in many places. I've traveled widely, mainly within myself, and that is how I've acquired the items in my museum."

It was the second time he mentioned his museum, so I figured I should be polite.

"What kinds of things do you exhibit there?"

"Oh, a great variety," he said. "Battleships, obelisks, massacres, animal concerts, hieroglyphics, conceptions of God, whirligigs, tea sets, circuses, lists of sins, plagues, Chinese shadow theaters, ambitions, zoetropes, voyages around the world, dictators, deep-sea divers, bicycles with no handlebars . . ."

My skepticism was clear.

Athanasius scratched his head.

"If I may say so, Miss, reality is just a matter of infinite longing. Right now, for example, on a street in Rome, you and I are exchanging pleasantries. It's summer. Vespas, like chrysalides, pass by. But who knows what you will be when you fall apart and find yourself."

The old man fiddled with his hands. It seemed like a blue delta opened in them, and that I had been in that delta once.

"It's entirely possible," he said, divining my thoughts, "everything is within our reach, always. And as for Emma," he measured his words, "she is in my Museum."

"Excuse me?"

"I mean, her work is in the catalog. Just like, if I might add, some of the dreams that were brewing in your country back then."

I shuddered.

"Listen," he added helpfully, "when you used to visit Emma, I would sit for hours in the stairwell, alone but for my copy of the *Musurgia Universalis*. I typically work *in situ* and travel with my mind, in that way, my collection spans infinite space and ubiquitous time. But it's hardly an accomplishment. I've done little more than embrace the fact that the world is me. Anyone could possess my collection. Even you, if you wished, if you were only open to the idea that each life is all lives, each era is all eras."

He spoke quickly, as if testing my intelligence.

"As you'll see, I've cataloged everything meticulously. The room that features you, Emma, and your friends is titled The Annunciation."

I cringed. Like when something is so far-fetched, like a poem, that you have no choice but to play along.

"At first," he went on, "I confined myself to observing the glacial perfection of the utopia that seduced you. I tried to determine how, and by what means, you all landed in that bear trap. Even the Union Lawyer, who seemed reasonable enough, became a slave to his convictions, which are just an antidote to boredom, so that his own views became his worst obstacle, they kept him back from what he fought for, something he had no name for. Forgive me, Miss, but of everyone who frequented that apartment, you seemed to have the greatest limitations. It was like you wore blinders that kept you from questioning things. For you, doubt was a weakness, so you closed your mind, to your own thoughts and everyone else's, opting for a literal, stinted view of things."

He waited for his words to sink in.

"No, *obbedire non è una virtù*. As for Emma, I'm afraid she didn't see things very clearly either. But, at least, she spoke out against intolerance. She was one of those people in whom the mania of revolution incites a rebellion against rebellion, as if her personal revolution were in favor of sanity. In short, she had no faith in the greater ends of politics, even as she held to her own ideal. I'm referring to her search for that elusive shade of blue."

I startled.

"Did you only know the people who *visited* the apartment?"

"No, no. From the stairwell, I observed the activities of everyone connected, directly and indirectly, with Emma. Humboldt, for example . . ." He cleared his throat in a calculating way. "I followed him many times though the university hallways, at the rallies, with El Bose . . . until one day . . . well, you know . . ."

"Yes," I said, and an immense fatigue washed over me. When I awoke, I was alone.

I saw a scrap of paper at my feet.

"Freedom is an inward pursuit, and art achieves it, because art gives life. Freedom is a kind of beauty. But art is still a transition, an untimely gift that has to conquer self-absorption on its mission of exceeding what we know and no longer needing anything."

I knew the handwriting.

"Emma," I called out, "are you there?"

The dark restored quiet, and with it, the mystery of human life, with its pretty mornings, futile battles, and words that tug at reality like magnets but also alter, mutilate, and annul it.

There's nobody here, I mused, but that nobody is Everything.

I folded the paper and, pocketing it, reentered the night, like some unthinkable terrain.

In my dream, Humboldt, El Bose appeared in his swimming suit, with his usual suntan, that whistle around his neck, his dazzling green eyes, and his ringing laughter. It was as simple as that. He sat next to me in the Caffè della Pace and took a blue notebook out of his pocket. *Un caffè latte*, he said. Or maybe, *fuggire, fuggire*. Either way, I know that he's come to find out what I've done with my life. Then you show up, out of nowhere, and tell me that you taught a history course using the novel *Bomarzo*. And I want to show him my poems, so I rummage for them, but there's nothing in my bag, and I'm practically about to cry when El Bose hands me the notebook, it's a gift, he says, I smuggled it here for you, so I open it, and then, out from under the tiny letters emerge, one by one, Humboldt, I swear it, alive and well: Black Fassano eyeing me like a benevolent crow, Duck in the instant he arrived at Ezeiza, Toni throwing punches like crazy, Susie blushing, as always, on one side of her face, Brains claiming he never bought a word of Socialist Peronism, Mousie hunched over like a little Duke of Orsini, and with him, Penguin, Bashful, Cripple, Filly, and Chester, a veritable Sacred Forest of Monsters, and all of them heavy weights, in the know, and Evita, who dropped her literature major—remember that?—because she said the meetings always devolved into a debate about whether the universe is a finite series of concentric spheres or a totality of worlds in eternal exile, and with all that nonsense, how the hell can anyone do anything that might affect the masses, because she's a practical girl, she says, not like Victoria who stuck with Lit and never learned the difference between the vast and the negligible, and The Ringer too, Humboldt, who went on doing his thing, and Indie who didn't do a damn thing to do in the first place, and Lieutenant who was a Military School cadet and never rode a Vespa or toted a helmet around the Campo de' Fiori.

Don't worry, El Bose said, there's more. Then I saw myself, Humboldt. I saw myself as if in a sequence of photograms, arrayed in what seemed like a magical merry-go-round revealing life for what it is, an illusory mechanism following its own rules, bringing us what it has to bring, everything, back and forth and around again, reinventing who you are, your name, biography, dreams, and all for what, and then El Bose looks at me, and facing the whole world, Humboldt, facing the tourists and *carabinieri* and swallows in Rome, he takes a shameless step into the air and starts to sing, cheerfully, *The waves, and the wind, zucundún zucundún.*

The monk was right: Emma spoke out against intolerance. "It's horrible," she would say, "the world reduced to good versus evil, the cliché that the end justifies the means, the Decalogue for a Democratic Activist, memos delivering orders, the countless reactionary writers no one's ever read. And would somebody please tell me, what the hell is *popular art?*"

Painting didn't really interest her either. What she did was copy, fastidiously, every painting of the Annunciation that she could get her hands on. She copied them in a fury, ravenously, as if by not having to invent her own forms, she could directly enter the unseen. She wanted to paint a work that wouldn't, in any sense, be hers.

"After all," she would say, "all artists just express the same thing under different guises. Why pile on more images?"

Her favorite painter was Filippo Lippi, because Lippi, she claimed, painted with desire. (The proof, according to Emma, is that he eloped with a pious woman from the Prato who modeled for him.) She could spend hours staring at Lippi's shade of blue.

Emma, and her orange hair.

"I just met a Union Lawyer, and I'm going to have sex with him," she announced one day at school.

She said it in one breath, as if startled by her own resolve, her wild fate, as if her body would produce, that afternoon, at precisely 3:30 local time, the next summer solstice, preceded by a lunar eclipse in quadrature to Venus, with Jupiter in the house of love, and so on.

Filippo Lippi's angel appears on the right of one of Emma's Annunciations. It has orange wings, one shade darker than its halo.

"Maybe that's love." Emma said. "Being bound by something you can't see."

Then suddenly, as if that color infested her, she becomes a wild conflagration, an intensity that ignores the limits of the seen and the visible, so maybe she can calmly sense, as when the world can't touch us, that truth isn't just one thing but many, that it lies hidden in our existence, and that to decipher that enigma is just as difficult (and here is one of the richest, most complex secrets in the world) as not to.

1972. First glimpse of the Turdera district: *If this isn't The People, where are The People?*

1973. Sonia swept the floors at the Student Union. The guys passed her around, from one to the next. *A la lata, al latero, al Tío lo defienden los fusiles montoneros.*

1974. A rainy evening, with a funeral at my heels, and you, or specifically, your eyes. Learning new verbs: to defeat, to die, to lie low, to execute.

1975. One architecture for morning, another for night. Words make useless inventions, or things are shadows that words project onto the world. Which of these two statements is true?

1976. Were you the comma that, when omitted, leaves the meaning deficient?

Then one day, with no warning, it is snowing in Rome. It is snowing, and I think: "Now, at least, I'll have a portrait of the winter." I wish I could just write a list, Humboldt, not to forget what was ours. Our parrot, Balboni, squawking on top of the fridge, your striped shirt, your invisible hat, the way you treated me inside those green walls, the full moon over the tiled patio, and your steps that left no footprints, the child in you, cast off, orphaned, back when it was safe to walk at night. And that dress I never owned, with nothing under it, when you walk in and look at me, like you have no clue how to look at me, and it doesn't matter that we're not alone, you whisper something dirty, your touch echoes through my body, my desire is carnal, bestial, the rhythm of your hand like a feral animal, and everything's a little wet, my eyes, my vile mouth, my senses pick up, loosen, I lower my head, I straddle you, I slip you inside me, all at once, all that glory, that terror.

It's snowing in Rome. It's snowing in the white city of second childhood, and it's as if silence fell over a nocturnal garden where Death can be seen strolling, guiltlessly, in no hurry, delivering the Good News of Life.

At what point does the phrase *they must have done something* elaborate perspectives around an absent symbol?

I'm talking about entrapment, as if from behind bars. (I'm behind bars.)

Tomorrow, yesterday, the day after tomorrow, I had a secret, but I'll never know it. On the other hand, I'll know, all too well, the theory of the secret I'll employ to explain why, in all probability, you are who you are, and why Rome (when I leave Rome) will still exist, why the river is the god of all water, and other uncertainties equally marvelous and sayable. (Only the imprecise is sayable.)

But I digress. Oh, Descartes, feed doubt, and you'll end up being a dirty bourgeois. I'm in the center of the Empire. All bridges are connected by water. Does Rome have a zoo? What is a stable object? I'm writing things that I shouldn't. *Humboldt loved you* has no meaning. There is no train departing for your vacant house. Tomorrow never existed, nor did the scores of stunned birds in Athanasius's museum. My memory invents you, lays you bare, caresses you, digs its fingers into your eyes. Childhood is a poetically unimpeachable place.

"You can't be serious," my Private Life said. "How many times do I have to repeat myself? How long can you keep romanticizing something that never happened? Try some phosphorus pills, for your memory. Maybe then you'll recall that you attended the French Institute, that you dressed in Marilú Bragance, that your name was always on the honor roll, that at the Naval Academy dance, a cadet in uniform led you across the floor to *Strangers in the Night*—yeah, you, who else? And don't say "so what." You have to accept, integrate, incorporate, conciliate, and reconcile the irreconcilable, though that was never really your forte.

And spare me the ridiculous questions, like: which is

the lesser evil, a woman without legs or a woman without a head; or which is better, the weapon of language or the language of weapons? Because these questions, darling, don't have answers, or worse, they only have wrong answers.

Let's stick to the facts. The fact is, you come home (so to speak), Humboldt is waiting for you, and the following exchange takes place:

'Hey.' Silence. 'What's up?' Silence. 'What's wrong?' Silence. 'I missed the bus, sorry.' Silence. 'Hey, I said I'm sorry, come on.'

Dialogue goes stale like chewing gum.

Later you replay it until you know it by heart.

Why not just put sticky notes all over the place, in the bathroom, on your computer, next to your alarm clock (and under a magnet on the fridge), to remind you? They should say 'It's over,' 'He did not rise to the height of circumstances,' 'One nail drives out another,' stuff like that.

Or what about visualization? Every time you imagine Humboldt, drag him into the trash. Then immediately *empty trash* and watch him get swallowed by the little can of virtual waste.

Do this without hesitating and, more importantly, without thinking, until you start to feel strong and silent, like Emma Zunz, and you're capable of saying: 'Goodbye, victim! Get lost, leave me in peace, I'm going to take down your story like a criminal file, I'm going to savor every line (no one talks about their misfortunes, however horrible, without enthusiasm), I'll work nonstop, no shortcuts, I swear, I'm blowing you a political kiss, I'm sending you a staircase of bones so you'll *never* descend from heaven, this is true revenge, a Roman notebook, glory be to Hate, glory be to Hate at eight o'clock, my dear, my darling rock, come on, go right ahead, mail me letters, you can even insinuate yourself into my dreams and drown my ears in morality tales, I won't care, I swear, I won't care, yeah yeah yeah

yeah yeah yeah.'"

The Union Lawyer. His reputation preceded him as a wanted man, a seasoned veteran. He spent a whole year in the can during the Argentine Revolution, and he wasn't ashamed to say it. Prison, he said (like Thoreau), is the proper place for a free man.

His perennial gray suit, shabby cuffs and collar. He had a wild expression, like he was always in a rush for no reason.

He's been flying under the radar for a while now, from meeting to meeting, back and forth, like a blind bird, against his own better judgment, though no one is the wiser, not even himself, and least of all Emma. She has started to live without any idea of why he leaves or when he'll come home, to love him in that grim way, as if he'd already been taken from her.

All of this from one kiss to the next.

He asks the same question, more insistently every time.

"What is truth?"

"The only truth is reality, General," Emma laughs.

"No, not reality, M'lady, I asked you about truth."

And at that, they each descend into solitude, as if diving for love, a shadowy object. That's their dubious method, in a world torn between ideology and tenderness, of listening to the things that go unsaid between them, as if tuning into another dimension where the things that never happen actually do, and what's so terrible about that, if life is an incomprehensible mechanism, sometimes cruel, sometimes beautiful, like the naval battle brewing in a heap of paper boats. Remember when you played with toys?

Had Humboldt been born in Rome in 1646.

Had he been less obsessed with degrees of consciousness, ideological coherence, the difference between a tactic and a strategy, the origin of family, property, and the State, the bitter power relations between the enemy camp and the people's camp, he might have asked himself:

What are the ideal geometric forms?

Is it possible to draw a navigational chart in an imaginary space?

Is there any link between the bark of a dog and the apparition of sunspots?

What color is the soul of the *Madonna del Parto*?

Stuff like that.

Humboldt can only stand well-formulated questions.

"But where do just ideas come from?"

"From the experience and systematic process of class struggle. If you want clarity, you've got to look to facts, not to figments of the imagination."

"But what's a fact?"

"Something that exists objectively and can be analyzed

in the frame of a concrete situation, while accounting for all the various factors on which it rests."

"But if what exists isn't fully in view?"

"Impossible. The very thought deviates from Mao."

"Did you see *La Chinoise* by Godard?"

"No, I'm a Peronist. Keep in mind that revolution isn't some drawing or embroidery or piece of literature, it's an act of violence by which one class defeats another."

"So what do you do for fun?"

"C'mon, cut it out. We're fighting to end the exploitation of the masses and imperialist plunder. Revolution means sacrifice. Plus, like Che said, it's all or nothing for a revolutionary with a righteous ideal. That's our most important possession, that's why we walk around with death in our backpacks."

"Oh."

Humboldt, I don't get it. All I do is ask myself why it happened, but I don't really know *what* happened, or maybe I just don't understand it, or it's beyond my grasp, and all I can do is tell myself stories.

Once there was, I tell myself, a sort of Perplexed Longing.

One day, this Longing invented The Word House.

As if by saying House, she'd really be saying a whole lot more—*I'm afraid of the dark*, for example, or *Mommy made me mash my M&M's*.

This Longing greatly admired The Unknown. One day,

she said:

"Death is my justification. The Unknown is like a god, I mean, you can talk about an absence like that forever, however long that is."

"But is there a word for me?" asked The Unknown. "A pet name, maybe? A sweet nothing, even just to whisper? Dear? Darling? Pumpkin Pie?"

Longing didn't really know. Either God begins in medias res, or God is a tiny golden fleck, invisible to the naked eye. But as for The Word House, she thought out loud, she's nothing without a house, and vice versa.

"Watch out," said The Unknown, "Even if The Word House has nothing to do with herself, she's really sensitive. If anyone mentioned it, she'd be devastated. Maybe take her out, somewhere nice, buy her a balloon, and later, when she's just about to fall asleep, break it to her gently, then maybe she'll accept it, and let go of her childish desire to possess things, especially the things she already possesses, and make peace with everything, and get her affairs in order, going once, going twice, gone, see you later alligator."

"What is the word *God* supposed to mean?" blurted The Word House, making her first appearance (though she really wondered about the meaning of the word *I*).

The Unknown and Longing traded glances. What nerve, they both thought at once. To burst in like this, uninvited!

"Can a name die?" The Word House pleaded. "And if a name dies, then does everything under the name die, too? And everything above it? And on the side? And down low too slow?"

What *is* it with you?" asked The Unknown. "Can't you just content yourself with *being*—as in right here, right now, in the world?"

This dialogue, Humboldt, could play in my mind ad nauseum.

As if nothing actually happened. ("Nothing ever happens," says The Unknown).

Irony is just sophisticated ignorance.

"Why don't you talk about Emilio Massera, or about Frantz Fanon's thesis that the worse off you are, the better?"

"I don't know. Living makes me nervous, living in Rome, especially."

"Well, no one would ever guess it, the way you flit around town, like you're on cloud nine."

"Hours rain down, minute by minute, but time stands still. Is this what people mean by *grasping what slips away*?"

"Beats me. We were so close to life, we mistook it for death."

"Do you remember the movie *We All Loved Each Other So Much*?"

"No."

"We saw it with Salvador and Negrita, at the Lorraine."

"Oh yeah."

"Negrita had a thing for Gassman's character."

"That figures. Negrita loved to be difficult. Gassman was a reactionary, that I remember perfectly."

"Where are you?"

"Not in that beat-up country, not a chance."

"And what about me?"

"What *about* you?"

"I can't see you, Humboldt. Did you die somewhere along the way? Or are you still on the run, in your broken body, holding your banner high?"

"Who knows, I could never really conjugate the verb *to run*. What's it to you?"

"It's seeping into my bones, this need for words to go back and reconstruct what never happened. Come back to life soon, Humboldt, I beg you, do it for me."

The music corresponding to this scene is *A Cure for Pain* by Morphine.

"What's up, man? Can't crack a smile?"

El Bose's dimple lights up his face. The café is empty. They can relax.

"I'm glad I ran into you," he says. "Talk to me, man, it's been ages."

Humboldt slouches a little, like he's carrying a load but doesn't know what.

"They're going to kill every last one of us."

"You've got to be kidding me. Come on, man, we knew we were risking our necks on day one. If you didn't, you should have. Did you already forget that ass-whipping at Ezeiza? I mean, sure, there were other factors to consider back then… the girls from Avellaneda, for starters.

Humboldt protests, begins a sentence with *The workers*.

"Give it a rest, man. *The workers* never so much as
pissed in our direction, that was all talk, toss me a cig, will you?"

Humboldt reaches over with a pack of Particulares.

He thinks: "Thousands of bodies jumping from tall
buildings, escaping across rooftops, tucking pistols under their
pillows at night. The Triple A is knocking us off, one by one.
People lying awake wondering whether they shouldn't just leave
while they can . . ."

At that instant, as if perfectly natural, as if a golden
stag flashed across the southeast entrance of Santa María Sopra
Minerva, he remembers a scene: she is leaving the bath. She
wraps a towel around her body and, with her bare feet on the
tiles, walks over to the azalea (which casts its shadow on the
poster of Evita) and stands naked, as if her innocence were
enough to cover her, or turn her into a tree, a fountain, a mirror
of the world's mysteries. Then something inside him clicks,
rewinds him to a silence even before silence, because any word,
at that moment, would be an act, and acts, as you know, alter
reality (even though they can't touch it). He lowers his eyes, as
if he had seen something he shouldn't, and swears to himself
that he'll always hold on to that memory of Earthly Paradise.
Then she leaves, like always, see you around, catch you later,
and in the space she leaves behind, cracked but symmetrical,
something leaks into view, and he can make out, for an endless
second, an image like motorcycles streaking across the mind of
a woman who, right now, standing in the middle of the street in
a foreign city, smiles and thinks, *We were just kids . . .*

"How about we play pretend?" asked The Word House.

"That's so unoriginal," said The Unknown. "Isn't that what we always do?"

"Let's pretend that right now, out of nowhere, Longing gets a letter in the mail."

"What will the letter say?" The Unknown asked.

"Excuse me," Longing said, "but if it's addressed to me, then I'll read it."

And without wasting a moment, she slips on her glasses.

Dear Longing, little mermaid,

How are you? It's a typical March night in Buenos Aires. From my window, I can see the universe, the neighborhood. Don't get carried away, it's nothing like the night in Pasolini's *Decameron*. I'm exhausted…I feel like I'm caught in a battle between social struggle and struggles of every other kind. The crisis is going strong. But, don't get too excited, hegemonic thinking is still alive and well, not to mention the Sunday ravioli and incessant soccer. Basically, nothing is new, but I've had this strange feeling. It's horrible, like I can't get enough air. It's taking over my life, I panic out of nowhere, and I'm never on time. For what, you might ask? Well, to my borrowed bits of prose. That's what I call them, because I copy them from a book, mix them up, and start playing with different combinations. The main thing is never to add my own words, everything has already been said, and more importantly, I don't believe in private intellectual property. What does that have to do with Peronism? Nothing. At most, I guess, it could relate to the *gauchoesque*, which is the genre that, in the Rio de la Plata, represents the writing of disaster, something like Romanticism played backwards to cast the national shadow.

Or if not, then with the tradition of the fragment, which is the consummate literary device. Either way, I won't deny that, at one point, I was a factory delegate in an area that didn't even show up on the city map. A guy I worked with told me that there was a center of energy right under our feet. Ten blocks away, inland, a foreign narcotrafficker had built, using only recycled materials, full-scale reproductions of European castles. One morning we stood on the roof of the factory (four floors up, in the middle of the pampa) and looked at the castles. I thought: The imagination is a delusion that staves off madness. Afterwards, I climbed down, and took the road of dreams, where artists like Malevich live, and all the others who never quite fit into the frame of revolution. You see, *carissima*, it was just a nasty case of sunstroke, but my trip to the roof gave me a poetics. Not national or popular or anything like that. Just a kind of excessive velocity, full speed ahead toward the past, where we discover what we were, even if just the outer skins that we keep casting off. Pay attention, this applies to you, little mermaid: your place is here, with your childhood, your stories, the ones you'll build someday out of dolls and aqueducts and silkworms. And the future? Where is your future? I'll leave you that impertinence, which won't sting as much as the present moment. I'll look for you, against all odds and the ruling class. They won't defeat us. Remember how they charged Malevich with being a *piccolo borghese*, but he never stopped searching for the zero of form. Don't be a stranger. Kisses."

"Not bad," Longing admitted. "Who's going to sign it?"

"The author," said The Word House, "*autrement connu comme,* your Emperor Très Noir."

El Bose yanked him by the sleeve.

"You remember Sérpico, right?"

"Yeah, that guy was a piece of work."

"We got things done, though. After the *Cordobazo*, we were unstoppable. Too bad we brought back our Old Man. . ."

"Keep it down. Sure, you can blame Perón, but we weren't exactly perfect either."

"You're preaching to the choir, man. I'm the one who spoke up when we did away with Rucci."

"He was a filthy prick."

"But that was fucked up." El Bose said. "And Brit was the only one who had the balls to say it. And as soon as he saw the whole militaristic craze coming, he made himself scarce. Remember?"

"No."

"You don't remember?"

Humboldt scans the café, as if determined to keep his foothold in reality.

"I don't agree with you. Ezeiza was a set-up. The Unions Act was the classic trap. Besides, thousands of people are disappearing."

"My point exactly, man. All signs point to the top of the organization…they're out of control."

"What are you trying to tell me? News isn't making it to my part of town."

"You're better off not knowing. It's all bad. The shit is pouring from all sides."

Humboldt vaguely nods. His hands tremble. His left temple starts to pound.

"Alright, kid, lighten up, you'll give yourself a heart attack. Let's change the subject. Did you get laid last night?"

Humboldt blushes.

"Well done, man, I knew it. And how was it?"

. . .

"Don't be such a jerk, come on, spill it. How many times did you give it to her?"

"Don't talk like that, man," Humboldt says.

"Why not?"

"I'm in love with her."

"Ha, looky here," El Bose says, "the typical horny kid from Quilmes, all hot and bothered."

Humboldt gestures for the check.

"Lighten up, man, I'm just yanking your chain. And by the way, shave that mustache, will you. You look like the fish food that keeps washing up in the headlines. Give me a hug, man."

How many books have I read about madness?

It's almost ten o'clock in Rome. Seventy-eight degrees. Summer. Crickets chirring.

No one will ever know what the present moment has cost me. In the present, I'm the one who is still breathing, still dying with every breath. I'm walking on crutches, as if learning to walk, I'm learning to walk. It's marvelous to walk in Rome! All of a sudden the dirty streets turn into a white silence, like a pristine garden of marble where a statue blooms, and that statue is you, or actually, the absence of you, illuminated. Summer looks perfect in writing. Perfect, because things never change. Right now, if I write "It is summer," then summer it will be, forever: crickets chirring. Future generations will come back for a feel of this pain, and someone will say, blandly, once there was someone, or one night in Rome, someone listened to crickets. Words as evidence of what is lost. A universe in mourning, where all unspeakable things tiptoe through the ruins.

Things never change. Like right now, back at the corner of Cabildo and Chile, I am still the woman you awaited that night, alert to every passing minute. If I don't show, you'll pack up the house, but here I am, standing there, with two packages burning in my hands, not getting burned. It's a conflagration now, I can see it, beside your statue in Rome (crickets chirring), and it will blaze forever, as long as it's summer, as long as someone is at war, just as we were, with their dreams. I keep moving. I keep moving through the streets of Rome where there are no sirens, where no one assaults any sort of regiment, where no one plants a pipe bomb at the police station or crosses a checkpoint with an explosive device. Emma quietly approaches, with a poem by the hand. This happened in Italy, too, she says—don't forget about Aldo Moro. An announcer ascends the platform. Applause. Ladies and gentlemen: *La notte rossa è finita, anche à Roma*. Nothing remains but the canker of summer. The poem, meanwhile, has finished its striptease and is now cavorting in the Trevi Fountain like Anita Ekberg. What a glorious Sunday, the announcer says, the canker was a small price to pay. Please give a warm welcome to the desperate poem entitled "Requiem from Another Country."

All the busybodies come up to get a good look, sniff around, take pictures.

How long ago did Tala die in the strategic counteroffensive? How long since his body turned up shot in El Chaco, where no poem would ever get wind of it? (Though the state got wind of it.) This was a war with reality, the poem recited, to clarify. Hallelujah, said the busybodies, they've massacred the images, now there's room for new ones, let's go skinny dipping! Emma walks over again, and I ask her: Can a poem bring bad luck? What kinds of poems are the most harmful? The overwritten ones? The ones that are too beautiful? Which poems should I have protected myself from but didn't? Which poems was I foolish to believe in? Emma doesn't answer. True beauty, like this image of you engulfed in flames, is always threatening. Several policemen wearing gas masks pass in front of the Trevi Fountain. I hear my name, or something that resembles it, or maybe one of the names that I've lost and no longer remember.

I still want to be the woman you loved, the target of your anger, fantasies, and lies. The one you were too fickle to keep. Crickets chirring: a book. I've wondered if delirium is just a refusal to consider suicide, or maybe, it's not having the energy *to be*, simply, naked in the water. Sirens crooning. A blind man yells, cursing the poem. Rome awash with summer obsessions. Summer, somewhere between art and passion. Who were you, anyway, Humboldt? How did you factor into my rebelliousness? Humboldt, shy of his sex, and me, naive to the taste between my legs. *I'm singing to you, so you'll come to be, my life.* All wounds are light, Emma said. And the main thing about light is, you can make it go blue, to cloak the dark.

I hereby declare my intention to commit suicide, as soon I finish writing the summer.

II.
On the Unknown
and Surrounds

That night, Humboldt, I waited for you in the house with green walls.

I was wearing my camel pea coat, and it didn't go with anything, not with the neighborhood, or the stink of the Riachuelo, or that sham story we came up with every day, down to the tiniest detail, to explain why no one came over, ever, no relatives, no friends.

Who knows why I put it on.

Maybe to deceive. Obviously the coat belonged to another world, a spectacular world of movie theaters, restaurants, and people walking around fearlessly. I'll make them wonder, I thought. At least for a second. They'll say that a girl like that, wearing a coat like that, couldn't have come of her own volition. She must have been abducted by aliens, torn from her family and dropped off here, in no man's land. (I thought so myself sometimes.)

I waited for you that night, eying the clock, for once grateful for the noxious stench of the Riachuelo, which masked the smell of ink.

When you showed up, your mouth spewed questions.

"Where did you get this letterpress? Who gave it to you? Did anyone see you come in? When were you planning to tell me about this?"

"I've got to run out," I said. "If I'm not back by 12, grab whatever you can and split."

I let the door slam behind me. I wanted to prove (to you) that I could overcome my fear. I walked out, ready to take on the night. The March rain hit my face, and I thought I heard a little voice, maybe my mother's, warning me that I'd ruin the coat. Outside, a rosy light, just like I've seen in Rome when it snows, reassured me. The unreal night would camouflage me, because I was equally unreal.

Mechanically I made it to the corner of Cabildo and Chile.

There wasn't a soul on the street. It was just me, in my camel pea coat, with a package under each arm. Another guy would smuggle them into the Tubomet factory in the morning. I looked at the clock. I stopped at my reflection in the glass, to be sure that the night hadn't erased me.

This is depressing me, Humboldt. Couldn't we just forget all the details and make up a fable?

Let's say a young woman is being punished and doesn't know why. On that first night, she swallows a pill and goes to bed. On the second, she repeats the procedure. But on the third night, she's determined to face her pain. And so, she cries all night and, at dawn, when she's totally exhausted, a messenger arrives with an explanation. The messenger is herself.

Or maybe, there's a castle and a village. At the determined hour, the castle residents, who are cruel and stupid, close their eyes to confirm that, when they open them, the world will be the same, while the people in the village, who are good and stupid, do the same thing, but to see whether anything changes. In this ancient rite, both parties forget that the castle and the village are imaginary and, for this reason, this story has no ending and its outcome is irrelevant.

The fewer words, the better. After all, nothing is gained by them, or even recovered. Like right now, I'm writing, but where is the cup where you poured your morning tea? Where is the clink of the spoon? The weight of the spoon as you lifted it?

Anyway, Humboldt, there's no doubting the mystery of the world. A word dreams about a spoon. Later the spoon tastes like lemon and goes out for a walk along the Via del Corso. Meanwhile life, I mean *my* life, Humboldt, grows weary, and a little hope flares up, because if I keep trying, if I don't abandon this inhuman effort, I might lose myself, and maybe, who knows, I might fall over fainting and find you there, halfway between dreaming and the dream itself, touching the air, like a king.

Rome, I'm *in Rome*, Humboldt. I need to keep repeating it.

If I only manage *to be* in Rome, then reality, whatever

that is, will come flooding back. Then I'll see ruins wherever I look: the world's loveliest staircase, the equestrian statue of an emperor, an angel guarding a river from a round castle, and a pair of dancing bears straight out of Fellini.

"That's right, Miss," Athanasius said, "there's no time like the present for discovering the reality of the unreal."

Who knows how, but there he was, the old man, helmet in tow, standing beside a Vespa. It was like something out of an altar by Luca della Robbia or, who knows, out of that scene from *Roman Holiday* when Gregory Peck sticks his hand in the Bocca della Verità.

"Let me try to be of some assistance," he said. "I know it's hard to remember, but you were at the corner of Cabildo and Chile, were you not?"

I reluctantly nodded.

"If your friend doesn't arrive, you thought, then no one will deliver the flyers to the factory on the following morning. And what if a Ford Falcon, speeding toward you in the distance, suddenly slammed the night shut? But that didn't happen. At that precise instant, unbeknownst to you, someone scratched an inscription into the tablet of your life, and that emblem opened the doors of Time, where you might find *The Book of Good Love*, octopuses, the paintings of Caravaggio, all questions with no answer, each and every motorcycle in the city of Rome, and perhaps even the name of wisdom, which is the rarest, or most subtle, form of love. Do you follow?"

Who was this man? What made him tick? What were his hang-ups? I noticed his weak frame, his thin lips. An almost-white beard softened his face (but not his gaze), and his forehead was wrinkled. I knew next to nothing about him. I knew that his books, which Leibniz had admired in his day, where full of illustrations that, under the pretext of scientific exactitude, had profoundly delirious effects. And I knew that connoisseurs regarded his Museum as a kind of Noah's Ark, a baroque encyclopedia, a grand monument to nostalgia—and also, no doubt, as the dream of a bulimic, a neurotic, an insatiable hunter of marvels. Maybe I would visit someday.

"Do you remember, at least, the friend you were waiting for?"

"Yes."

The old man scratched his head.

"Well, when he finally came, there was a problem, he said, I can't take the packages, you'll have to wait an hour, I'll be back at midnight, meet me here. His tone was military. Then you started to walk. Something ominous pulsed in the air, with the weight of certain ideas you'd never dared to entertain. Humboldt is right, you said to yourself, they're going to kill us. Worst of all, my life means nothing to this guy. Then you saw, like a flash, a bus pull up. You took it. Without a moment's hesitation, straight for your house and the smell of ink, and the men looking you up and down, any of whom might have been a cop, and with *this* on you, you thought, two thousand incendiary flyers written and printed by you, yourself, cranking the machine all day nonstop, until you finally got off the bus, and crossing a vacant lot, in a motion that resembled prayer, as if God were watching (He was watching), you got rid of the packages, first one, then the next, without stopping to think, because certain things in life have to be done without thinking, and Humboldt was waiting for you, and that night he held you, for a long time, in silence, because he understood, without even

a word, that you'd brushed with death, you of all people, a girl who
didn't know the first thing about death and, for that reason treated
things, even the most serious things, like games. That embrace,
you realized, was a pact, which neither of you should break *ever*,
because it united you against sadness and defeat, and the beautiful
dreams you'll have to learn to replace, as if you'd been banished
from childhood, little by little."

Something is coming back to me in Rome, Humboldt.
Something like a *Vita Nuova*.

With a satisfied expression, Athanasius handed me a fat,
yellowed folder.

"I'll leave you with this catalog of my Museum," he said,
"in case it might be of interest."

He took a slight bow and vanished into thin air, but not
before rapping his feet a few times on the cobblestones.

I just stood there not knowing what to do. In the
distance, Vespas buzzed like insects past the Ponte Fabricio. I
opened the catalog and read:

Museum. Temple of the Muses. Catalog. Objects placed
by category, according to evident internal logic. Each piece
is glossed and complete with an explanation. Visitors should
acknowledge that all things come from God and return to Him.

—Two spiral helices, curled to overlap
—An organ that can mimic the songs of 1,600 birds
—The Oracle at Delphi

—Two bells that toll independently
—The general principles of mnemonics as established by the poet Simonides
—A Sanskrit grammar manual
—The dove of Archytas showing world time, including astronomical, Italian, Babylonian, and Ancient
—Several clepsydras from the temple of Isis or Iseum
—Several unmapped cities
—An interview with Huidobro
—A viridarium
—A treatise on women and dolls
—Another on suicide
—Another on the expression *I don't care*
—The *Rosetum Exercitiorum Spiritualium et Sacrarum Meditationum* by Jan Mombaer
—A *thesaurus eloquentiae* that lets you build palaces with syntactic structures
—A Russian perpetual calendar
—A tabernacle with a Palermo Annunciation
—Hero of Alexandria's theater of automata, just as prized as the tragedies of Euripides
—Meaume de Brugge's obscene postcards
—Several toys dreamed by Joseph Cornell
—Ten versions of the Book of Revelations
—Some of the Stagirite's scattered formulas
—Euclid's meridians
—A Renaissance opuscule on courtesy, lust, crime, and feelings
—Two glosses and a commentary on Kleist's Marionette Theater
—The anamorphic ceiling of the San Ignacio Church in Rome

—A mirror that favors metamorphosis
—Another that duplicates the star of Bethlehem
—Another that repeats votive erotic sonnets, intended to grant
or request favors
—Another that allows the image to flee its object
—Another that reflects another mirror which is the world,
according to *The Meccan Revelations* by Ibn Arabi
—Another that permits the representation of anything one desires
—The mirror that Archimedes invented to defeat Marcellus
of Rome
—Cagliostro's mirror, which reproduces a swallow ad infinitum
—The deadly mirror of Narcissus
—The mystic mirror of Meister Eckhart
—The one in the *Roman de la Rose*
—The constellated mirror of Paracelsus
—Mirrors dreamed or owned by Faust, Gérard de Nerval, Marie
de Medici, Pythagoras, Cocteau, the Lady and the Unicorn,
Newton, Macbeth, Solomon, Swedenborg, Monsieur Teste
—Other mirrors concave, cylindrical, misleading, miniaturizing,
esoteric, broken, liquid, abominable as the mirrors of Tlön,
useful as the ones that allow the hunting of the tiger according
to the *Bestiary* of Saint-Victor
—Alice's mirror, showing the invisible, i.e., death
—This museum

The list of objects goes on forever.
The world and its music boxes.

"Are you okay?"

"I'm calm."

"Good."

"What am I going to do when you leave, Humboldt?"

"You sound like a broken record."

"Didn't we learn something? Was it really a total loss? Was the fire real, at least?"

"You never know."

"Where are you right now?"

"In the same place as always, getting closer to the world, closer to you."

"When I finish writing this, will they take it all away from me? Will people say it never happened? That I made it all up?"

"You can't take nothing from nothing."

"So then, you didn't leave me? Were we innocent? Didn't they ask too much of us? Didn't we pay too high a price?"

My questions clang together, contradict each other. Humboldt could never think about more than one thing at a time, so he doesn't answer.

For a second, he looks like he's crying.

Image of solitude.

Radiant.

There's no musician who corresponds to this scene, but the music keeps playing anyway, like in a photograph or a dream, and the music is sad, very generous and very sad, like writing that flings itself, eyes closed, straight into nothing.

On Practice, by Mao Tse Tung:

If you want to know the taste of a pear, you have to chew it. If you want to know the properties of an atom, you have to conduct experiments. If you want to know about revolutionary theory and methods, you have to participate in revolution.

Therefore, the first step in the process of knowing is sensory contact. The second step is the synthesis of sensory data, developing concepts. The third step is concrete practice that, based on such concepts, enacts changes to reality.

He who foregoes personal participation in world-changing practice is not a materialist.

Yet this process is not immune to contradictions and pitfalls. One could argue that it is endless because, from the eternal flow of absolute truth, men only extract relative truths, and in addition, in the objective world to be transformed, you have to account for all those opposed to such transformation.

At the current stage of social development, history has granted the proletariat and its party the responsibility of knowing the world and transforming it in a *correct* manner. "To err, persist, err again, and persist until Victory" should be the motto. In China, the process of transforming the world has reached a crucial juncture, and we can finally see the darkness dissipate, clearing the way on Earth to a luminous world as never before seen.

"What's wrong?" asked The Word House.
"Nothing. Did you see the last Labor Union report?"
"No, what does it say?"
"I'll read it," Longing said, slipping on her glasses.

"We will not forget the thirty-four senators who voted for the impunity laws. They are sycophantic traitors to the nation. They have insulted thousands of starving children, patriots who gave their lives for the country after the British invasion, and all martyrs to the national cause, the victims of June 16, 1955, the people shot in José León Suárez, the thousands murdered and tortured by the military, and all who died in the Malvinas. They are vile scum."

"So what's the problem?"

"I don't know, it's Sunday, I might be a little depressed."

. . .

"Did I tell you that I saw a poem naked the other day?"

"No sweetie, you didn't tell me."

"It was talking to itself."

"What was it saying?"

"Just running its mouth, I guess: Where am I going? I'd like to love myself all by myself. Is it healthy to hesitate?"

"It doesn't sound very clear-headed."

"Who knows. The best part, though, was that it started to tell me a story. Just like that, without my asking, without even pausing to offer me a seat, it said: Once once once upon a time there was a revolution."

"Not a bad opening."

"Yeah, but there was a kind of tantalizing cruelty in its mouth. I could detect a real hateful streak."

"And then?"

"Nothing."

"What do you mean nothing?"

"Nothing. The poem tried to justify itself by saying that poems have no plot. Then it showed me a basket full of red words, and I noticed that death, which stood at its side, had an aura around its shadow."

"Oh."

"Do you know what *exum* means?"

"No."

"To walk around in a fluster, according to Pavese."

"And who, may I ask, is Pavese?"

"Someone who wrote poems he didn't need to write."

"If Pavese were alive, would it. . . ?" The Word House meant to ask, but stopped in the nick of time.

"What if we plan another Return Operation?" she proposed.

"But no one wants to return."

Clearly, Longing was depressed.

"Let's stop pissing around, people," thundered a lanky guy known as Nobody, making his debut. "Perón will return whenever he damn well pleases."

"Who's this loser?" asked The Word House. "The police force superego?"

Ideally, thought Emma, I'd paint a painting of a painting, an Annunciation not set in reality, but only in the reality of another Annunciation.

This transpired at three in the afternoon on a certain March day in the apartment on la calle Uruguay.

At 3p.m.: Inspiration wavers. You feel a tightness in

your chest, then the overwhelming urge to be irreverent. Like: not to paint, just *to be*. A body, the wind hugging your waist, an act cruel and blind as any passion, betting double or nothing, hello, goodbye, what's your name, I'm the invisible girlfriend, delighted, do you happen to have any matches, thanks.

At 4: Blue appeared. *That* blue. Unadulterated quiet. How I'd love, thought Emma, for that blue to be a portrait, my own still portrait, and to be able to contemplate myself in it, and for the portrait not to be dead.

At 4:30: She glanced anxiously at her watch. If I were on campus printing propaganda, she told herself, I'd just be altering the balance of power between the center and the periphery, considering the most reactionary sectors of the Movement, mounted on the politics of Lopez Rega, et cetera. It's hard to paint, she thought, when you're listening to the roar of the action. I'm sick of action. What's important is what I can't see, and to trust my impulse to paint a mirror out of that blue, a pure vision.

At 5: Actually I can't stand action. Its violence inevitably desensitizes us. Distracts us from the mysteries in ourselves. I prefer art, where everything, always, refers to something else (one blue to another blue, and that blue to yet another), so you can never quite frame it, you can never make it 'official,' like rain or a sunset can never be official. Nothing worries the people in power, nothing threatens them, like the freedom that lies at the end of what we can put into words. More than anything now, I want to step outside of the shelter of the law and the danger of opinion. I want my paintings to get emptier and emptier, to feed the fire that lights the world.

At 6: What if politics was just a dream that reality exists?

At 7, On the verge of exhaustion: Art is like death. Inevitably, you lose yourself to both.

In Rome now, with a wide grin, El Bose is sporting his green tee shirt and lifeguard suit.

"I've been thinking a lot about Sonia—did I mention that?"

"Ah, what a girl. She'd jump into bed with everyone, remember? Political work, nil, but a great ass."

El Bose talks into my silence, occasionally glancing back to check that I'm still there. (But where could I possibly go in this relentlessly circular city?)

"By the way, kiddo, wearing all those layers, you look like an onion. Only Humboldt could have pictured you naked."

...

"But joking aside," he continues, "political practice has taught me a lot. Utopia's a sham, and if you want to get there, no crime is great enough. And all that business about the new man and his female comrade is a load of crap."

...

"Anyway, I'll always like my nickname. The King of the Acolytes, remember that? I really did have a way of bringing in recruits, especially the girls."

If El Bose had been born in 1646, he'd have learned that there are eight rings rotating around the earth, in each of which a siren stands and sings her own notes in counter-harmony with the rest. He'd have learned that it's dangerous to drink water that comes from snow, that there were no fig trees in Paradise, that there are forty-two languages in the *Books of Authority*, and that the scarab of matter unfolds in helical form and always returns to where it started.

El Bose grinning, showing his dimple, and a flicker of gold.

As if happiness were possible.

As if it were driven by desperation and the breeze.

Dear Longing, little mermaid,

It's after eleven in Buenos Aires. I just finished dinner and had a panic attack. Don't get me wrong, things here have their ups and downs. Take my week. On Monday I surfed the Internet, then the power went out. On Tuesday, I was burning up in my apartment, so I took the car for a spin. I drove out to the country and spent a lovely afternoon on some kind of Macedonian farm—sadly, though, protesters closed the road on my way home, don't even get me started. On Wednesday I woke up feeling a little dizzy and strangely nostalgic for the pine tree we had in our yard when I was a child (the one that trembled with fear, like me, whenever it stormed). On Thursday I shut myself in my room and worked all day. On Friday I went to a demonstration, nothing too exciting, just a bunch of people doing their own thing, political solutions *niet*. On Saturday I went for a walk and ended up in a park full of women wearing horrible Etam dresses and showing their children a love so primal, so foreign to the philosophy of history, it literally made me itch. Then today, before I knew it, it was seven in the morning, and even though it was early, I already knew I wouldn't be going anywhere. Happy Sunday, I thought, I'm half in reality (as usual), why not write a letter to my asymmetrical friend.

Poetically, I admit, I'm not doing much. Sometimes I doubt I'll ever write again. I'm a sort of jobless employee of the Absolute, waiting for a sewing machine to walk by holding an umbrella. But my new *machine poétique* is my car. Since I got it, I've been racing across the edges of this precipitous city like I'm in Verne's submarine. I don't miss a thing, not the sulfur in the streams, the plays on words, or the poor children's palace-homes dreamed up by Evita. Too bad tomorrow is another day, and I'll have to face the dread of being a decent citizen in a polis overrun by cardboard pickers.

You can probably tell, little mermaid, that I don't belong to anything, least of all to the bureaucracy of third-rate intellectuals who've never heard of Cotard. True beauty is the stuff of magic spells, I try to get to it in the same way I strolled through Paris as a child clutching my father's hand, back when I had a pet iguana, which I later set free because it broke my heart to hold it prisoner.

You know what? I've been thinking of names for you: My Lady of the Lake, My Ruin, M'lady. Which one do you like best?

Now I'm picturing you making a thoughtful expression, totally defenseless, under a crystal bell. Would that be love? Well, it's about time.

Want to start a *clan enfant*? It could be something like a national cathedral of life. It wouldn't be half bad. I love dodecaphonic operas of thought.

I'll see you later, in that distant past, on the only date that might have made us happy. Goodbye, *il mio impossibile*. Distance is a ruthless countess, let's avoid her at all costs!

Geometrically,

Your Emperor Très Noir.

P.S. I came upon this line by Enrique Molina: "There were always dead men and strangers at home." Isn't that great?

See, Humboldt? Everything is happening more or less as I predicted.

Just like I thought, the moment *I love you* entered the story, it would be summer, around the hour of the siesta, when the body, lethargic from the sun, longs to be kissed from the waist down.

At first you'd be only an emotion, the sum of points in space that chance to unite, like everything that is and dies. Your absence would help to disarm me, to bring me down to a human scale where fear doesn't have a name even though it's more real than reality, because from that low point, and only from there, is it possible to rise to another kind of light.

I thought, practicing my loops and hoops, like a woman *truly* in love, I might break the bars of perfectionism and stop rattling off lies like "In the garden of the night, a nightingale was singing." After that, a train longer than my life would chug away again and I'd start to *truly* experience the miracle of things, i.e., I'd stop being *me*, so that I might become something I've never even imagined.

But, I'll admit, it's pretty slow-going.

I can't understand who you were and, for that reason (there must be some reason), I can't get over you, even though some might say that I played my cards and played them well, and that time is on my side, and that because I'm in Rome, I've already crossed the Rubicon, *Alea jacta est*. They might say this, even though everything else seems to say, unambiguously, horribly, the exact opposite, and I go on like someone who has never been born (like people who are forever unborn), and your absence is a hole stuffed with random crap, like a Piranesi print.

The other day I nearly dropped to my knees in the middle of Rome and proclaimed my desire to quit living. I had imagined you with another woman. She shifted like lightning. First she was me, then someone I didn't know, then the blonde who fluffs her hair and giggles ha ha hee hee like one of those girls delivered by Providence. The whole ordeal made me spin, and I almost lost it. My fantasies had never pushed me that far. I rummaged through your pockets, searched your papers, listened in on your phone calls, like a typical nervous wreck. I missed my dentist appointments, stopping reading the headlines, I even stopped asking myself whether it's more important to write or live. That day, the desire for sex hit me like never before. Like a light that gets brighter just before dying out. My mother's predictions are coming true, I thought. Her words have needled their way into my body like a vulgar tattoo. I almost phoned to congratulate her. It's not easy to convince a body to be alone, unsatisfied. I'd never felt such a sharp sensation of *failure*. My abandonment was total, infinite, concrete: right there in front of me stood the other side of myself, and nobody was there. My mother got what she always wanted, and I was lost in Rome, like any other automaton, taking inventory of the ruins. That's when I heard you say *History is written by the victors*. You said it dogmatically, the way you always talked when you were afraid. I thought it was impossible for so many bad things to happen at once. Not only had I lost you, but I was going to have to accept the fact that I was the sole, absolute, exclusive author of my misery. It seemed too late to take it all back. Wasn't I putting terrible, ephemeral, incredible words in your mouth? I'm sure that my style made my desperation perfectly obvious, but that desperation never worked its way into my hands (not to mention yours). Maybe this was the price I had to pay for writing. Byron's words rang through my head: "Of all bitches dead or alive a scribbling woman is the most canine." Then I remembered how you walked out on me. He left without saying goodbye, I repeated, almost triumphantly. That should be some consolation. Not to mention, he never knew how much I loved him, like he was some kind of Prince Charming, in that pointless way that women love when they haven't stopped being girls. If only you'd understood, Humboldt. But you didn't understand, and I didn't have the nerve to tell you. Between my naïveté and my sexual corset, I had two fears: that no one would notice me, and that I'd be too noticeable. How pathetic! I said. Without even realizing it, I'd reached the fatal juncture in our relationship, and I still didn't know what 'our' even meant. I was stuck. Your silence brought me to the faintest version of life, waiting around for nothing. (What is *that* feeling called?) I interrogated my pain: Have I achieved the impossible and lost myself in the process? Am I dead, too, but I just don't know it? Why, every time we kissed, did he get farther away? I don't want to go on, I repeated at full volume in the heart of Rome, I don't want to be the sole survivor of this story. That night I dreamed that the two of us skated over a brilliant white ice rink in our wheelchairs.

"I feel lonely," Longing said. "What am I going to do? I'm so in love!"

"Who is he?" The Word House asked, alarmed.

"How should I know? I'm in love with emptiness! I want a morning full of red thoughts, a little wooden rocking horse, the TV series *The Invaders*, floating arrows, all of that stuff, but none of it, and even that isn't enough, because as soon as I want it, I don't want it anymore, am I making any sense?"

"It's clear as crystal, sweetie, everything that ends, ends. . ."

"I had the *worst* dream last night," insisted Longing, who hated over-simplifications. "I dreamed that my mother came to visit. She brought over a video. The video was blue, with some flashing images of Rome. Your exile has already begun, she said. And that upset me so much that I started to bleed, an unstoppable hemorrhage between my legs, and I just stood there paralyzed like a tree and bled, frozen, half-dead, slowly bleeding.

"Take a deep breath," The Unknown interjected.

"What if we call The Soul? She's got to be around here somewhere," The Word House proposed.

"You think? But isn't it a little late for that? We're already on page 52."

The Soul didn't keep us waiting. She came in a flash, without making so much as a peep, and huddled in a corner.

How serene, to see her, just being her.

The Word House, no doubt profoundly moved, took a seat and began to recite, for her own sole benefit, a never-ending story.

Once upon a time, there was a word that died of *l'inconnu du désir*.

Maybe I'm not *myself*, said the word, who also
answered to the name House. I mean, the fact that I go by
House in no way implies that I actually *am* a house. Because,
without venturing into too much detail, a plain old house is
obviously not the same thing as a staged house, a house under
siege, a house named by a prisoner under torture, a pink house,
or even worse, a white house. Basically I'm a natural dissident,
pure and proud, and here is my story:

One day I was riding a sled on a Russian steppe.
Or maybe it was a farm in Oklahoma. Or a five-star hotel in
the middle of the Cordillera. *Un véritable rêve du Paradis! Un
horizon carré!* White snow buried everything. Everything that
passed over it left deep tracks in time. Then someone came and
delivered the good news: Away you go, Miss! And then, as if I
understood the categorical imperative, I shot through blindness
like an arrow and dreamed, in succession, that *a)* I was on the
plane of observable space and time, *b)* I was in the vast stellar
abyss, because this world continues into the next, only the
direction is reversed, *c)* I wasn't anywhere, and this happened
twice, in duplicate, and *d)* everything I couldn't see was actually
me, in other words, my utter confusion, otherwise known as the
world.

Then the past went blank, and I started running
around in circles as if, in spite of everything, I'd been there
all along, until finally, one day, I stumbled upon the grotto of
marvels and became a collector, I began to piece together scenes
and invent music to accompany them, without realizing that
in reality all I wanted was to hunt down every single synonym
for every single word I knew, and that's what I did, expanding
my vocabulary to astounding limits, but even then I was stuck,

I couldn't get beyond myself, I never found the infinite kernel of my desires, so I kept swinging back, as if after a long absence, to that generous and empty, empty and generous, hole in the middle where all stories come from, but not the house, *hélas*, not the house that hides in the word that I am, infinite and tiny as the world.

You were right, Humboldt, reality isn't my forte. I never knew what to make of the vendor on the corner or the lady who lugged her enormous handbag past our house every day on her way to buy bread. But this is too much. I spend my days, hours, straining to remember, and nothing. I arrange all the dates on the table, complete with names and events, and I still can't unravel when or where it all happened. Which refrigerator did Balboni's cage sit on. When was I hired at the syringe factory. Who gave us the azalea that used to cast its shadow on the poster of Evita.

It would be impossible to reconstruct that scenario.

But which scenario, I wondered? I'd gotten rid of everything, Humboldt, right down to President Onganía's first name, don't laugh.

Now my job is to desecrate words. I work at night, when no one can see me, cloistered in my room in Rome. What could it hurt, I assure myself, if the words were ours to begin with, we invented them, we waged war with them, the same way we made memories out of them.

Oh, Humboldt, I'm obsessed with patching together unlikely things, while in reality, what do details matter in life? What had to happen happened, and whatever still has something to teach us will happen again, by another name, over and over, and who knows what's happening now, as all these Roman girls whiz by on their Vespas, with their helmets neatly in place and their purses securely fastened, not to lose their lipstick, as if nothing that we did back then even happened. The distance between us is greater than the space between celestial bodies, and yet any of them, Humboldt, any single one, could stop now in front of me and hand me something, something like a coded message, *avanti bersaglieri*, for example, because in the Big Sleep there is no kingdom, no object, no place, nothing that isn't labelled with the tetragram of God's name, and all of that, in spite of our pathetic memory and your stubborn disappearance, which returns to my side now and whispers in my ear *Grow up.*

My dear...errr... Longing,

Guess what happened? The other day, I ran into Emotion. What a lunatic! She vanishes the very instant she asks herself: *Riddle me this.* What would I feel, what could I feel, and maybe even acknowledge as a feeling, if I only knew I was feeling it?

I greeted her tenderly, not to startle her. She glared back at me with suspicion, like a platinum blonde automaton from Transylvania. "Where have you been?" I asked. Solitary confinement, she replied, my favorite spot. Then I added, very softly, so that only she would hear: I've founded a theater of sadness, I belong to nothing, and on March 11, 1976, I had a panic attack. The city was vacant, except for one good-natured dog. He looked at me with an air of nobility and told me that, sure, the crisis is pretty terrible, but the meanness of humanity is much worse. I tried to hear him out, but all I could think

about was how some things seem more plausible than others.
If I tried, maybe I could write a book that captured the forest,
Huidobro's *Altazor*, the 20 truths of Justicialism, and the giraffes
at the zoo. The dog furrowed his brow (as if dogs had a brow) and
suggested that I move to the suburbs, that I take up residence
in the Futuristic City of Children, it'll be your Abyssinia in the
pampa, he said, your own no man's land, and you'll even be issued
a toy, care of the Evita Foundation. So that's what I did. And so
we died, happy ever after (the dog and me), dining on partridge
until Life did us part, under a lovely crystal cemetery.

I left her pretty shaken. You think I did alright?

As for you, I've decided to send you a few borrowed
bits of prose, to see what you think. I should preface them by
saying that the real idea behind these fragments is the fragments
themselves. There's no message to hunt for, not even in the last or
first lines. My writing is staunchly pro-revolution, but wary of all
the big words, and it tries to acknowledge the price we pay and
the realities we cloak when we use those words. Needless to say it
doesn't put a lot of stock in victorious causes, and for that reason,
it formulates painful questions that tend to distort things, fairly
or otherwise. I don't like to feel constrained. My dream would
be to have my fragments in some Museum of Heterodoxy, some
collection of elliptical and difficult texts, resistant to hierarchy and
category, with ambiguous limits, but arranged to accommodate
wonders. In other words, a bunch of little boxes that describe the
labyrinthine paths where infinite human desolation lies in wait.
It's kind of ambitious, I know, but doesn't the idea of a fantastical
and philosophical museum strike you as brilliant? It would be like
a book that would last a lifetime, and you could toss in all kinds of
facts, thoughts, abstractions. Anyway, let me know what you think.

Next time I'll tell you how to transition from utopia to a default state, and how it's possible, even crucial, to delight in reality, which is just a great big nothingness full of forms, even if you have no idea what militant form goes best in that nothingness.

Be good and write back soon, don't leave me waiting, remember that I'm very, very longing, too.

I miss you, little mermaid. It's not easy to find people who are smart and a little complicated but aren't in love with themselves and don't think they're perfect.

I'm sending you my sensation of being lost, my slips of the tongue, my desire to write without knowing what will come of it, like I'm inviting something to happen that has already probably been said somewhere but went unheard, all of those things mixed up, with no rhyme or reason, plus thousands of kisses for my *amica lontana*.

Your Emperor Très Noir.

P.S. Don't forget that the impossible basically boils down to what we lack a desire for, and like Camus said, "One must imagine Sisyphus happy."

Seen from afar, everything is white, desperately white. A few heroes, even better hidden than the night itself, even more awake than the night itself, running here and there, saying goodbye to their dreams, marching and waving flags. The rest is dark (I know what I'm talking about, I swear).

That thing over there, swinging back and forth, is my heart. It doesn't suffer from vertigo, but it stares in the direction of the secret. What tiny feet! Does he want to return to my breast?

Fucking weather. The sea (not visible in any direction) is choppy. No one can sail across. "I don't want to stay," says the captain of the ship, "it's no fun here, come in the car and pick me up."

Characters, all somewhat villainous, enter. "We spook the civilians," they say. "What a pretty trade, military life!" The dawn startles. Something flies overhead. Oh, no, it's not an airplane, it's something white. A white idealism! A white sorrow! A white death!

Let's not assume that the die is cast, that the battle has begun, that something cruel and restless muddies the air. Pick your chin up, be as chipper as a little lad with new shoes. "But now it's bedtime," Daddy says, "maybe tomorrow the sun will shine on us."

I often walk along the Via Giulia, Humboldt.

I walk parallel to the river and wait for you at the end of every sentence.

Meaningless sentences like, "A pebble lies on the flank of an avalanche" or "A dark girl, drifting through cold air and questions."

At night, I dream that you return home like a wounded soldier. Sometimes I wake up to voices screaming, Murderers! Murderers! but I can't see the attackers, I only see myself, and I have a gaping head wound, I'm bleeding to death. Other times, tear gas grenades are flying, there are group arrests, mass killings, daily raids, and it's every man for himself. Then the Via Giulia is flooded with searchlights, and at the end of the street, a vendor sells religious postcards marked with the insignia of the Black Cross, and this time when you come up to me you're toting a leather briefcase and I greet you at the front door of the house of writing, I tell you that I hate it when you look like a bureaucrat, but I kiss you anyway, I close my eyes (to avoid looking at the briefcase), and the kiss would never end were it not for My Private Life bursting in to say: "*Quo vadis*, babe? Didn't we agree that this guy was history?"

Daytime is no better. I hit the gym, run some errands, show up to work at an office where nothing ever seems to slow down, nothing except my image of you in your olive green sweater reading the paper with Balboni making a ruckus on top of the fridge.

So this is my life, some of it written, another little bit left to write, and meanwhile according to *Il Corriere della Sera*, horrible things are going on in the world, senseless violence, massive attacks, and maybe we should actually take stock of them at some point, if democracy survives. It's amazing, history happens twice, Humboldt, the first time as a tragedy, the second time as a parody, and in some cases, revolution is the most reactionary thing of all, according to *Il Corriere*.

Do you get it? I don't. I have to admit, though, that I'm terrified by the magnitude of this crisis. I wouldn't want to be a historical subject again, not really. I don't want them to be able to say: "They ran and set fire to mountains, they moved rivers, they persevered amid darkness, they fell to the ground like birds under duress, their horses crumbled into the mud." (Nobody has said that about us.) Still, I go to protests with the young people in Rome, no matter what they're against. All demonstrations are the same. It's always the same fury, the same violent, erotic shiver through the crowd. I'll never get over my fascination with it. I still push my way up to the front. I hold up a banner. I wish you could be here, Humboldt. This time, maybe you wouldn't be kissed by death. Maybe in the middle of the Via Giulia, we'd be enlightened.

Focus on the searchlights.

Searchlights, like ships that can't decide which waves to cross. They waver like a dagger in the night. White night of the hunt.

Why this procession of shadows? What's behind these quiet presences in the Realm of Emotions.

Oh Humboldt, something is growing larger as it recedes. You.

"Do you remember the movie *The Sheltering Sky?*"

"How am I supposed to remember if we never saw it?"

"We didn't see it, but we *will* see it—remember?"

"I think so. Why?"

"Because, at the end, this guy is dying of malaria in Morocco, and the girl, who barely has the sniffles, starts to freak out. Then he consoles her and promises that he will never (never, did you hear that?) abandon her, that he will take care of her until the very end, even after death. Then she quiets down, and the poor guy dies, just like that, a fade to black and a little sign that whimpers: The End."

III.
Perón Is Dead

This is one of my favorite versions: Humboldt and I started a family.

He was a clean-cut gentleman in a suit, and I took up poetry like a game of marbles. The romance (with poetry) was short-lived. I woke up panicking in the middle of the night, not knowing who I was, Baudelaire or Beautiful Dorothy. The same thing happened with Breton and Nadja. That was my worst dilemma. I poured all my time and ambition into it, I enrolled in classes on feminist theory, and then one day a green-eyed blonde came along, and poof, he left. "Do you think you might have neglected him?" my mother asked. She had a point. When I read Baudelaire, I'd transform into a feline, a harlot, a libertine, and I'd feel like I was curled up on the poet's lap, while in real life, I'd be furious if a man even looked at me. How can a poet have a woman's body? Humboldt and I were a lot alike, or so a psychiatrist once told me. We were both laced a bit too tightly, and we had opinions about everything: how to live, how to kiss, how to work, how to avoid hypocrisy. Two true soldiers of Perón. No, I never ironed his shirts. And then, one

time, I cried at a meeting. El Tano had called me a goody-goody.
It was true. Whatever the orders, I recited them like a parrot. I
had rational explanations for every outlandish thing. Humboldt
took me in his arms. Like me, he preferred to be blind, devoted,
and loyal. Revolution was, above all, a test of faith. But no one
bothered to warn us that faith, at times, is just the outer ring of
delirium. Holding me, Humboldt thought of a solution: We could
politicize a neighborhood. By some stroke of luck, we got the go-
ahead, and Pepi gave us the contacts. When I mentioned that the
neighborhood was far away, Pepi asked: far away from *what*. We
joined up with Ophelia, Pedro, and Durval almost immediately.
I couldn't believe some of the people out there, how they refused
to open their eyes, how they hardly gave us the time of day, some
of them didn't even offer us *mate*. That got to me. I'm not sure
when I wrote my first poem—or more accurately, I don't know
when I *knew* that I had written a poem, which wouldn't have been
the first. I began to think about consequences. So did Humboldt.
Maybe that was how we wised up. Poems? What poems? People
mistook his denial for my independence. He was my political
mentor. I was in love with him. But I never told him how much
I admired or desired him, I wasn't submissive. A political activist
isn't a whore and doesn't want to be. Neither is a poet. Later I
became friends with a man-hater and wrote off Baudelaire as a
misogynist. She looked down her nose at me for sleeping with
the enemy, and Humboldt asked me if I was sleeping with her. I
am walking the edge of the abyss. I am dipping my fingers, my
red nails, in blood. I taste it, and it's my own dried blood. Maybe
this is eroticism. My psychiatrist recommended Alplax. After that,
whenever I cried, I'd start to yawn and drift to sleep. That went
on for years. You're right, Humboldt, I was never very generous.

I figured that being a woman amounted to loss: of time, of opportunities, of any hope of being like Baudelaire. I never wrote you a love letter, much less a dedication. I would have been mortified. I never played dumb, giggling and tossing my hair like the green-eyed blonde of Providence. I'm sharpening my words. My love is a knife now, and it wants to sink to the bottom, ruin everything, scream, confess the worst things like a torture victim coughing up her love for her torturer. I never apologized to you for anything, and I won't start now. You're a cold woman, my mother said, unfeeling, even you said it. So be it, I said, poetry is an ice palace. There the Snow Queen lives with her kidnapped child. The little boy puts together a puzzle made of ice shards, which are also the letters, the blind alphabet, of Desire. She promises to set him free if he pieces together the word *eternity*.

"How confusing," Longing sighed, "to compare writing to a game of marbles."

"And besides," The Word House added insidiously, "marbles is a game for boys."

"Pipe down, ladies," said The Unknown, "why don't we focus on the story? Keep in mind that nothing has been said yet, nothing that's *actually* real and not just made-up."

Longing and The Word House traded glances.

"What a downer," Longing whispered, "He reminds me of Nobody."

The Word House's eyes glimmered.

"Let's ignore him. I propose that we be really mean. Don't they say that the imagination closes a door but opens a window? Oh sweetie, my problem is that I'm getting more anti-*yankee* every minute. I can't swallow the IMF's shit, it's fatal. Yesterday the paper said that 'They are on the path to becoming another Haiti.' *They* are us! I'm completely anti-globalization, *chérie*! If I weren't so addicted to perfume, I'd propose the Cuban model."

"What are you guys talking about?" The Unknown asked.

"Nothing," Longing blushed.

Longing was always a little girlish, even in her slower years.

The Word House grabbed an aerosol can.

"*Soyez réalistes, demandez l'impossible!*"

Then she started to hop up and down. "Anyone who doesn't hop is Anti-Peronist!"

"Perón has died," the radio announced. "He has entered History as the Father of the Country, Head of the Nation, Strategic Leader of the Movement, whose greatest champions were and will always be the working class. The people," the voice said, "who hold up his banners, will rise again, with the strength of millions, and carry his name to victory." We rode in a blue car in the rain. Soft, insidious rain. The sky is Peronist, I thought, that old son-of-a-bitch. "A National Hero," according to the radio, "departed this life today, Monday, the first of July, at 13:15 local time. It is an immeasurable loss." And you, since last night, staring into space. All the funeral pomp, our massive demonstration in Olivos, our black flags, our lukewarm repentance, our nagging fear that we were too quick to abandon our father. And now, of all times, a new world record for disgrace, he dies on us, I thought, and leaves us to our own devices, like some refugee camp, some Incredible Army of Brancaleone pretending to repair a spaceship with wire.

An outbreak of indignation stops short at your eyes. All the oligarchs are celebrating, you say, look how chipper they are in Barrio Norte. Requiem music played on the radio to herald his death, the actual death of Perón, this is a disaster, I said. I watched out the window for a place to buy black ribbon. You didn't talk. The day dragged on. We had posters to print, groups to organize, columns to form, safety issues to address, people to feed, a tide of travelers from every corner of the country, and not just students and young people, there were old folks, children, entire families, all ready to brave the rain and see the body at any cost. Black Fassano gave out orders, a litany of specific tasks, cordons surrounding and protecting the demonstrators, the middle ranks wearing armbands embroidered with rifle, lance, and the five-pointed star. Comrades, comrades, he spoke on the steps of the University, this is a political act, we can't just hand the body over to the Right, we need a show of strength, we need to prove that we can mobilize. People wept. The bitter poverty of the community. Destitution in the rain. People have once again crossed the Rubicon. This is how we fell in love, Humboldt. Like you, I walked up and down the line handing out coffee. A million people. A million people with photographs of the shirtless leader, in full uniform, riding a pinto horse, embracing Evita, or huddled under Rucci's umbrella, getting off the plane. We need to reach the Congreso. We need to witness the coffin draped

in red velvet. Erase the memory, above all, of his face behind
security glass in Murderous Plaza de Maya, where he sent us to
die as the crowds jeered *Mon-to-neros, damn it!* Five blocks of
funeral garlandry. The rain wouldn't let up. What an absurd rally,
I thought. Our General has died on us, they said, who's going to
defend us now? The Peronist Trade-Union Association and the
62 Organizations entrusted with the catafalque in the mortuary
chapel. Hey, a student shouted, the people's organizations brought
him back, thousands of them died or went to prison for that, and
as soon as he gets here he turns his back on them, starts parroting
The Warlock Lopecito's lies, it's unthinkable, man, it would be
unthinkable anywhere.

 Street fires in the chill of this death.

 Fires in the cold night of the headless nation.

 The undisputed leader of the Movement is dead.
The strongman, fugitive tyrant, aging puppet, exiled president,
molester of teenaged girls in the Secondary Student Union,
catalyst of popular unity, chief, interpreter of the masses, who once
stole away on a Paraguayan gunboat, genius of class conciliation
and the third position, the pro-fascist, author of *The Organized
Community*, *el Pocho*, in sum, our man, is dead.

 People cross themselves. What now, guys? Everyone,
strap on a black belt and meet on the university steps. We left
under sheets of rain. Your jacket was jasper gray. Your armband
meant you were mid-rank. For us, his soldiers, you thought, Perón
isn't dead and never will be. We marched for hours in the rain. His
body rests in the Blue Room of the Honorable National Congress
under the banner of death. Our destination is the Congreso. The
line's stagnant, and it's getting dark. You and I sit on the wall of
a flowerbed at the Ministry of Education. I say something. I like

you, I think. You turn red. A few images assail you at once: a girlfriend, a glass jar, a rope with an inextricable knot. Crowds all around us. Everyone so similar, poor, desolate. I'm going to ruin his life, I thought. Thanks to Perón, said a woman next to me, we got the bricks to build our house. Another guy argued, under his breath, so people wouldn't hear him, that we have to be consistent, we cursed him two months ago, and now that he's dead we're just supposed to forgive and forget? Our people work tirelessly. We're like some kind of University Coalition for Solidarity with Popular Mourning. I turn to you, but nothing. Any minute, I thought, his silence will swallow the two of us whole. And the funeral flag flutters overhead. And the fire to flush the cold rain from this death, your kind of sadness. You slowly straighten your jacket, offer your hand to help me up, and say that maybe we could go to the movies sometime.

"It wasn't what I expected," said Humboldt.

"Take it easy. It's no big deal."

"It's just that, this time, things were serious in the can."

"What do you mean?"

"I mean, they hammered me. They wanted details, every name, how we connected, the whole batting order at the Student Union."

"Go on—and then what?"

"Then nothing. All that questioning, and then they just kept my ID and let me go."

"Shit, and now of all times, with checkpoints right and left."

Humboldt looked mystified, as if his last few words gave out on him.

"Ok. But, hey, you got out, right?"

"Yeah, it's a miracle, I don't get it."

Suddenly El Bose seemed to recall something.

"What exactly did that wacko girlfriend of yours do?"

"Nothing, she waited for ten minutes, and when I didn't show, she split, to work on a flyer."

"What was on the flyer?"

"How the hell am I supposed to know, Against the Brute Force of the Antipatria . . . Rifles, Machetes, something ridiculous like that."

"What did you do when you found out?

"Like I said, I got mad, I stormed out."

"No good, man. Head back to your place right now and give your woman some intensive rehabilitation, whether she likes it or not. Doesn't she know what it means to be an *integral* activist?"

You could see El Bose's dimple. And his green eyes, like those little colored bulbs they always hung, lifetimes ago, at the carnival."

Humboldt thought: "Shit, I froze. Why couldn't I tell him what happened?"

I was in the middle of spray painting *What's up, General?* when suddenly they surround me, take aim at me, order me not to move, it all happened so fast I couldn't even see the guys on lookout, one of the cops pointed his gun at me, he shoved me up against the wall with the butt of his FAL, I felt a potshot right here, and before I could even react I was in the backseat of the car, pressed between the two of them, then the driver peeled out, eyed at me in the rearview and asked them if they'd frisked me, the guy on my left says no, which really pissed off the driver, what are you, idiots? And he's about to stop the car but the one on my right says keep driving, so the driver speeds up and asks me if I'm armed. It's a short ride to station 17, but I've got time to think a million things, when will my friends realize that I'm missing, will she clear out everything at the house, what if they put me under executive jurisdiction, or even worse, what if they offer me the 'option' and I have to leave the country for good. I was scared shitless. I had a horrible feeling that Sérpico was going to walk through the door of the station and recognize me. Then I'd be finished. I went before the commissioner. His office had two armchairs and a small couch covered with green plastic, all sticky and greasy. The commissioner's a pig, he reeks of shit, but I don't have the courage to look him in the eye, which hits me like a revelation, fear is stronger than I am, and I notice that a cop with an unholstered gun is rummaging through my jacket, my pants pockets, they confiscate my watch, my cash, my ID, the commissioner flips through my address book, he asks me for my name, what do your friends call you, he's playing good cop, trying to sound paternal, I know you're a decent kid, he says, one of those kids who speaks at meetings, goes to rallies, not one of the ones who kill in cold blood, I pray that he'll keep talking, to buy me some time, but instead he goes silent and just glared at me, not adding anything, and I said that people call me Humboldt.

The commissioner was sitting on the desk, and with his left hand, he was puttering around with the stuff they dumped out of my pockets, I don't know if we stayed like that for an hour or a minute, in situations like that you're slow to react, you move cautiously, you watch your words, you just focus on how you're going to get your ass out of there, and then he finally said, don't you have have anything you want to tell me, anything about, anything about what, I ask, well, your friends, your girlfriend, what girlfriend, I ask, and the commissioner smiles, like he's a step ahead of me, what do you mean 'what girlfriend,' your girlfriend, the girl you've lived with for a year, I don't live with any girlfriend, I lied, I just stay here and there, sometimes I crash with friends, sometimes I'm in Quilmes with my folks, he's playing dumb, the guy with the gun interrupted while cleaning under his fingernails with the edge of a key, he thinks he can pull one over on us, what kind of morons do you take us for, *shh*, the commissioner orders, don't treat him like that, can't you see he's just a kid, just a little schoolboy, he's shy to own up to anything, but we can help him, he's probably thinking he can cover his ass with political prisoner status, said the one with the gun, don't give him any ideas, Lopresti, don't give him any ideas, can't you tell that he's just a sweet little canary, look kid, let's see if we can't understand each other, we can plant a whole fucking arsenal in your house, who are you trying to fool about not having a girlfriend, I strongly advise you to tell us everything right now, if you don't want trouble, better yet, let's take your deposition right now, Lopresti, get one of the non-coms over here to take down a statement from the detainee, if you tell us how, with whom, and for whom you work, I'll personally guarantee that you'll be cleared, but if you don't, I'll have to push for the most serious charges, then the one with the pistol smiles and adds, I'd like to see you then, and he gets up and leaves, not before tucking his piece under his arm. I'm finished, I thought. I thought of her, she must be afraid, and the thought flooded me with guilt, I just had to keep quiet long enough to give her time to tell the higher-ups, I played dumb, what I needed to do was to tire them out, somehow I'd come out okay, then a guy walked in, did you bring your typewriter, non-com, affirmative, and right then and there, he took my fingerprints, first one hand, then the other, and he started to type diabolically, but who knows what he was writing because the commissioner was the only one talking, he kept asking his insidious questions, but I didn't answer, I was quiet, like an idiot, keeping my eyes lowered, staring at the mortadella sandwich that the non-com had left by the typewriter, give him time to answer, said the commissioner, until at last he signaled something with a gesture, and the one with the gun shoved me, first to a courtyard full of uniformed men in shit-kickers and bullet-proof vests, but not all of them, some of them look bizarre, almost like they're disguised as us, and for the first time ever, I see them dressing like we do, in suede boots and plaid shirts, and then we go down a flight of stairs into a hallway with stripped walls, lit only by bulbs that dangle from electrical wire, where a standing guard asked, How bout this one? before they shoved me into my assigned cell, a sinister rat hole, no air, no light, and the guy with the gun told the guard, keep a close eye on this one for me, and then he said to me, don't even dream about getting out of here.

   It must have been maximum security, because not a minute later, I started to hear smacks, kicks, and screams coming from nearby, 'on your knees, you son of a bitch, hands behind your head, you fucking Red,' nonstop for hours, I have no idea how long, and the poor guy never stopped groaning in agony, he must have been writhing on the floor, now you're going to eat your own shit, motherfucker, and I was shaking because nothing good can happen in a place like this, and suddenly I had a crippling need to be with her, all I could think was how I wanted out of this story, it didn't help to imagine how they'd all be mobilizing for me, spraying graffiti, dialing numbers, holding emergency meetings, what the hell difference does it make, I thought, I was choking on the nauseating stench of piss, vomit, a lack of oxygen, and screams from the adjoining cell, I felt like I was suffocating, like they'd crushed my lungs, heart, stomach, squashed all my organs together, and I couldn't stop panicking, even when, at one point, the guard came up and made small talk, he was a good person, he said, he had a wife and kids, and what we all said about cops on our propaganda wasn't true, he'd never beaten anybody or ordered anyone to beat anybody, he just followed orders, and we should go after the politicians, not people like him, and even then all I could think about was my fear, my bones ached, I spent the whole night like that, I told myself it was over, everything was finished for me, and what am I supposed to do, I thought, what the hell am I gonna to do now, what the hell can I do.

"Do you have a story?"

"Actually, sweetie, I've be writing a lot…it's almost

finished!"

"No, dearie, a *story*."

"Oh sorry, I didn't follow. A mutual friend from school introduced us ages ago at the Petit Café."

With an alibi like that, we're screwed, Longing thought, but she didn't say so.

"Did you see? she asked. "Another letter came for me."

"No, let's have a look! Read it, what does it say?"

Longing slipped on her glasses.

Dear Longing, little mermaid,

I just discovered something. Poetry isn't *a gun loaded with future*. Poetry isn't a gun, period. How can something be a gun when it hurls itself blindfolded toward nothing, and just when it's about to reach the edge, one, two, three, jump, it turns a triple somersault, looping through the air.

I don't know. I had insomnia last night, and the idea came to me. When I can't sleep, the most irreverent things run through my head. Last night, they were mostly questions. Whose voice speaks in my borrowed bits of prose? Does the voice belong to anyone? Does it only belong to itself? Does everything exist only to arrive at one blank and perfect book, a book that writes itself? Stuff like that, pretty dismal actually.

Have I mentioned that I'm writing from a medieval castle in Umbria?

You'd love it here. The air is thick with a Giacomo Leopardi sort of misery, the perfect excuse to indulge in the world of high ideas, not in the lowly life of the polis. Plus, my face is like stretched leather from all the sun, like a child who has been playing outside for too long, so I inspire a bit of sympathy in people, with my face like a little orphan who has lost his world.

Speaking of kids, I have something funny to tell you. In the castle, there is a group of little terrors, a mini-mafia of marbles players. The next time I see you, I'll tell you all about how they lured me into their game. It was easy, really, because I had no idea what I was getting into. One day they called me over, stamped all my required visas, and in a panic, I just played along. I froze, which is always what happens to me when it's a question of a desire versus a reality. In disbelief, I sat down in a chair and said: "It's OK, I'll sit this one out." But Death is playing, too, one of them said, as if trying to convince me. Here, let me introduce you, her name is Beauty and Happiness. He said it with a feigned innocence he couldn't quite pull off. He was petting a swallow that he held in his fist. Go figure.

Apart from these *extemporaneous meditations*, I'm doing alright. Even though I'm waylaid in memory which, as you know, in our case, amounts to a covert prison. Little mermaid, it isn't easy to remember, on these gloomy nights, that we are, like it or not, simply *deixis*: the lack of a subject isn't enough to erase the gravestones holding fast in our imagination.

I bequeath them all to you, those battles for the past!

Then on the other hand, there's pleasure, little mermaid ... Pleasure is a completely useless passion. Never resist it! At any cost! Not even, and mind my words, when you're tempted to write!

The important thing is that one night overtakes another, and that you abandon your line of defense, though you're not big on metonymy. For the time being, I'm sending you a few gentle prods like sighs of grace. I miss you tons!!!

A ton seul Désir.

Your Emperor Très Noir.

P.S. When I get a chance, I'll send you another infinitely random dream about those marbles players. Kisses, lots.

"What now, Humboldt? How are we going to live?"

"Just by living."

"But you won't be there."

"I told you before, I'll always be there. And my words, unlike yours, are actions."

"Then the future did exist?"

"The future is the same as the past, just a little slower going."

"What was our plan?"

"That tomorrow would be *something other than tomorrow*."

"Were we right?"

"No. We had to learn everything all over again, the world, the question *for what reason*, what things are worth."

"Will we be happy?"

"I got lost sometimes, and you were never there for me."

"You weren't there for me either. You'd just say *I do what I can*. And now I don't even know where to find you."

"The way you lived paralyzed me. Your coldness was stronger than I was."

"I don't get it. Were you too late to arrive at who I am? Am I just desperate for something I'm about to lose, something I don't know how or where to find?

"More or less."

"It's so complicated! And what am I going to do when Providence snatches you away?

"You'll take a deep breath, pretty yourself up, and step outside for some sun. Life doesn't move forward in words."

"Oh, Humboldt, I'm going to learn how to sleep naked, I swear. Someday I'll make peace with my body. Pray hard that the happiness won't scare me to death."

The music that corresponds with this scene is *Pulse*, by Steve Reich.

Now pay attention. Hold your breath like you're about to fly a kite with blue ribbons against an identically blue sky. You have to keep very steady, because of the gleam in Humboldt's eyes and his hands that are incapable of fumbling, Oh how I'd love to have a bicycle with shiny new pedals—can you ride with no handlebars? Come here, let me show you, the glimmer in Humboldt's eyes and the heat from his body, one hand suddenly lost under your clothes, I'll play you at ping pong, at tag, at cards, now Humboldt and the grand canal of her, who ineluctably answers yes or no, with her heart held high, like the moon on its bier, as if it could rise as high as truth, when time swings back and forth and space is a mouth opening to another mouth, with eyes clenched tight, quiet down a little, and in this boundless game, Mother Goose, the little hidden cards, I'll trade you one with sparkles for two regular ones, Little Red Riding Hood and the wolf at long last in the secret of the forest, someone, from the street below, is calling, how ill-timed, as if they could answer. And in reality, one March, in a room in Rome, not far from the Porta Portese—how could they answer? You have to keep very steady. You have to pray that nothing will interrupt this dream that flashes in and out, at the heart of the world, like a salamander sizzling on an erotic TV screen.

"What is a bureaucrat?"

"A little tough guy, a sellout, someone inside a power structure who betrays everyone at the grassroots and never, or almost never, dies a natural death."

"And the Organizational Command?"

"A death squad charged with holding in place, by force, the politics of the metallurgical country."

. . .

"Don't give me that look, man, it's not that big of a deal. I mean, this is dangerous shit and there are plenty of guys who want to run home crying to their mommies, mostly the ones that come from money, but thousands of us are ready to give our lives for a country that's free, just, and sovereign, at any cost, no matter what."

"And do you have a lawyer to defend you? I mean, just in case."

"It's not a question of lawyers, man, it's a question of balls."

"And what's the dictatorship of the proletariat?"

"Forget that Bolshevik shit, we're Peronists."

"And what is worse: Imperialism as the peak of capitalism, or its supporters within the Movement?"

"It depends on the stage, on the tactical progress or pull back of the most representative popular sectors, on the state of the class struggle at that particular moment (beyond your desire to force reality into a box), on the development of revolutionary experience, on the deficiencies in popular organizations, on the anguish of participating in the national liberation process, on the international context and on that great Argentinean who *knew how to conquer*."

"Oh."

"A Quilmes Imperial."

"I'll have a tea with lemon."

When the waiter walked away, El Bose said in a low voice:

"Shit, I forgot to bring you that *Descamisado* you lent me."

"No worries, I don't want to have it on me when I cross the bridge anyway."

"You heard about Bocho?"

"Yeah."

"Unbelievable. He up and dies in the john from a gas leak, and right now of all times, when they're doing us in right and left."

"He deserved it for turning on Perón."

"Come on, man, you mean he never subscribed to Perón's bullshit. That's not the same thing."

"I mean that he was a lazy anarchist punk from day one."

"But you've got to admit, he knew a hell of a lot about the Russian Revolution and basically all of Marx by heart. He was like a one-man Central Committee."

Humboldt thinks: Focalist, left-wing Guevarist, mama's boys in the Movement For Socialism, El Bose is distorted because of his privileged background, I want to go home—am I going nuts?

"Who told you anyway?" he asks.

"A guy I know from the area got the intel. Then he adjourned the meeting right there. Anyway, when you think about all the scum Perón dragged in, and the reactionary factions of Peronism gaining ground, and the poor stiffs the Triple A tosses at us every day, who the hell cares...All I know is, in Zona Norte, tempers are heating up. The Columna Sabino Navarro is splitting up. Documents get to them, but not to us, man, they treat us like idiots: they order us to shoot in the name of some ghost politics, and if they had any idea how freely and inorganically we were talking right now, they'd ax us, no question, maybe even put us on trial, you've got to renounce your past mistakes and all that bullshit, because the whole premise of revolutionary violence, man, doesn't agree with this bourgeois crap, sons of a fucking bitch."

"Are you finished?"

"Yeah."

. . .

"OK, you have a point. Better to talk about my little rendezvous last night." El Bose's face lit up.

"Stop messing around."

"No, I'm serious. Last night was incredible. You know I'm pretty hot-blooded anyway, right? Well, I was with this chick, and she was tough, not just some bimbo, we got into a fight and she put a cigarette out on my back, and she wouldn't stop screaming, and my hands started flying, then hers, and then I all of a sudden, I couldn't see a thing, it was wild, man, we rolled around eighty times, like we were in Finland or something, not in this backward country."

Humboldt made a quick gesture with his hand, I have to go, I'm running late, as if to erase something, something he couldn't put into words, and not because he didn't know how but because the words for that feeling don't exist, c'mon, man, El Bose thinks, don't get so worked up, want to walk for a few blocks, the words for that feeling don't exist, you'd have to start running around in circles with love and commitment and the new man, and even then nothing would change, Humboldt thinks, standing up, which way are you headed, and he'd still be far away, very far away from his body's longing for her, conflating what he doesn't know how to give with what he doesn't know how to ask for, and conflating what he can't ask for with what he doesn't know how to take, and then the waiter hurries over, as if they'd called him, and Humboldt says, we'll take the check please, and El Bose looks over as if to say sorry, man, some other time, if you like, we can have one of those talks like we used to have, hey, remember making Molotovs, cooking up potassium chloride raviolis and filling all those little bottles with gasoline? Yeah, he says, but let's get moving, there's a creep on the corner, we'd better cross, did I tell you El Tano skipped town? What do you mean? Where'd he go? How should I know? To New Zealand, for all I care, I guess he couldn't take Bocho's shit, wait don't turn around yet, that's what we all should do, man, hop the boat and stop putting our asses in the fire with all the labor union thugs.

"Why do you always paint the same thing? I asked her.

"I don't really paint the same thing," Emma said. "I don't really paint at all. I just look for things that don't have names."

"And this one, what's the title?"

"It doesn't have one yet, maybe I'll call it *Study in Favor of the Hypothesis that God Exists.*"

"Can I have it?"

"What do you want it for?"

"I don't know."

The painting offered me a vague consolation.

Emma would have probably liked the idea of consolation as a function of art, but I still kept it to myself.

"You know that Humboldt thinks you're an elitist? He says that you should paint for the people, not for . . ."

Emma stopped me cold.

"I don't give half a damn what Humboldt thinks. I don't paint for anyone. The next time you see him, you can tell him that for me. If anything, I paint for the experience of painting itself, for the pleasure of it. See if that clicks with him. And I try to enjoy every last bit of it, that's why I start from scratch, like I'm blind, trying to break my old habits of seeing, so that something that can really come from nothing, so some free eternal something, like a rock or a maple tree, can emerge."

"But there has to be a bridge," I objected, "between the beautiful and the just."

"I don't know, and honestly, I don't care. I don't want anyone to have control over what I paint, much less to dictate to me what I *should* paint. I've told you a thousand times that I can't stand utilitarian ideas about art, and all that nonsense thought up by so-called promoters of the common good who don't understand that painting *is* thinking."

Her face was flushed, and it seemed like a dangerous idea shot through her, because she waited a little while to speak and, when she did, she spoke slowly, as if giving herself time for it to sink in.

"You know what? I've always thought that art is never contemporary to anyone. Like it's standing, by definition, on the curb across the street, disoriented, brushing off everything that tries to pin it down, because pinning down is always the foundation for domination. And that's how it works, whether or not it's trying to, against authoritarianism. Anyway, I was never a big fan of the morality of taste. I prefer fugitive gestures that lead us into the depths of ourselves and resist interpretation, sparing us the disgrace of realism. Do I even need to add that art is its own reality, and that the true measure of truth is depth, not accuracy? A work lays images over places that lack reason. If the world had more clarity. . ."

There was a clinking in the lock, and Emma jumped.

There he was, towering in the doorway. Lanky, disheveled, with tattered shirt cuffs. The Union Lawyer.

"Are you alright?" Emma asked. "Did something go down?"

He didn't answer. He just smiled, and it seemed like an

image streaked past his face, the face of a very old little child. Maybe a toy train, I thought, bound for the Sahara, and in the Sahara was an oasis, fiery orange like Emma's hair—Emma, who obviously could no longer see, hear, or think.

Time to go.

I'll leave them there, fully clothed, a little timid in the face of happiness—undeserved, of course—because, who deserves that kind of happiness?

"So it was," said Athanasius as he sat down beside me, "I can attest to it."

By then I was used to the monk's abrupt appearances, and to his disappearances which, at times, lasted for months. He came on and off, like a nonsense signal. Maybe he's the world, I thought, and he inhabits only himself. He *is* appearance and disappearance.

"That night I sat in my sleeping bag in the stairwell. I saw you leave, Miss. I even said *Bona serata*, but you couldn't, or didn't know how to, hear me. I remember it perfectly because, at that exact moment, I closed my eyes and heard someone call out to me, but by another name: Parmenides! Parmenides! Of course, I didn't answer. If he'd only called me Mister X or Edwin or Domenico, I would have looked up and said, Are you speaking to me? But Parmenides—and to top it off, in the middle of March, in that cemetery-city overtaken by a mysterious blindness, making it hard, if not impossible, for me to collect pieces for my museum. All I gathered were the fragments of a very unlikely whole: a ring made of tin, a perforated skull, an alarm clock, a half-packed suitcase, a pair of burnt testicles, that sort of nonsense. You waited for the elevator. How sad, I thought, but then immediately afterwards, how marvelous, because hardly a few feet from us, apart from everything else, even from the one who called me Parmenides, someone was rushing over to someone else and, in that precise instant, with the slightest of gestures, almost imperceptible, was spelling out a secret for all to see, between the stars and Konya, as if saying *eppur si muove*."

Shit, El Bose thought, I blew my one chance.

I know things have changed. Back when we occupied the university, we had a lot of time on our hands, we didn't work much, all the chicks threw themselves at us and we hardly noticed, we were too busy running our mouths about weapons and politics.

We'd even hit the beach in the summer, groups of us, staying wherever we felt like it, we hooked up with other people like us, fired up about the Movement, too, and there was a euphoria in the air, I remember that high, that thrill, when death seemed like a fascinating game, something very far away, and everyone was expecting Perón to come back, and when he did, the military would have to eat their shit. We had no worries, we were cocky, nothing was a big deal. As for the cops, they were always on alert, jumping at every little thing, but they were nervous, nobody could run the country, it was the perfect time for us to join forces, the shops would lower their blinds when we walked by, who cared if there were assault vehicles packing heat in the alleys, that Molotovs were flying over our heads, later they'd climb those tall yellow flames shouting Pe-rón Pe-rón, and we'd just run off, unstoppable.

But that was before, Humboldt. Shit has been getting to me, too, you're not the only one, we're all in a hell of a mess, those of us who didn't split, people cutting deals, it's disgusting, of course you, in your area, don't get wind of any of this, the workers aren't confused, you say, with people like them we can't go wrong, the guys who pissed around at the cafés really got to you, the guys getting their nuts off in the couples lounge at the Politeama, the way they chatted about art theater films, it made the bile spit from your eyeballs. I mean, you're a scrappy bastard from Quilmes, you'd just as soon jab a knife in anyone's jugular, probably mine first of all, if we hadn't been friends. All the potheads, like Toni, dirty hippies, you called them, who scratch their balls all day and mooch off their parents, typical lowlifes, maybe you were right, I've never been sure, but anyway, that's all history now, it hasn't been a joke for a while, and poor Toni is missing in action, like it's a war, and who would have ever guessed, after seeing him on the front lines swinging chains at those commie morons in the Purple Stripe. Too many things just don't add up, man. Rucci's corpse washes up, the Montoneros declare themselves illegal, and as for us in the grassroots, we're left holding our dicks in front of the death squads, and just guess where we're going to have to stick our slogans now. It's getting down to every man for himself. And don't try to tell me it's the leadership's job to rise to a higher level of conscience in anticipation of the next phase. However you look at it, it's a shit bath, and soon enough, it'll be a bloodbath, but what's the point in telling you, you just sit there and take it, even the heaviest shit. How can you seriously keep talking about a coup? Saying that when the masks fall off, people will see who the real enemy is? You were always kind of a Trotskyite, but you're way off the mark here, man, you sound like someone from the Bolshevik IV International. Bocho was right: Perón played us, then he turned around and called us a bunch of kids. He threw us to the curb, and you don't see it, you go on and on about the *true* Peronists, and the working class, and meanwhile everything is going to hell, even the dogs are scared to walk down the street, the undercovers don't dare to go outside, there aren't any more assault vehicles or boats or patrol cars or civil services from the Secretariat of Intelligence, López Rega's ultra-fascists just come up and slaughter you in broad daylight, and Perón is going to kick the bucket any minute now, and then you'll have to go and shove your goddamn Peronist Hymn straight up Carlos Gardel's fancy ass.

The world is inside me, Emma thought that night, as she watched the Union Lawyer sleep beside her.

It's inside me like a fallow garden where, since the beginning of time, The Mirror of Simple Souls has shone.

And yet, I'm nowhere even close to finding that image that expresses nothing, and whose empty forms, endlessly multiplying, let us see.

What is the world, I wonder, as seen from a tree, a bridge, a swing? Or from a consciousness that deliberates, solely and exclusively, about how to remain silent?

I'd like to paint a music of objects, a sort of sonorous

tapestry of eternity. That music, resisting some of its own possibilities, in its reticence, would be like a night bird or a beacon of small ships sailing across pure time.

Better yet, I'd like to paint myself with the music of being. Maybe then I'd find shelter in what we call homelessness and make peace with death. It doesn't seem all that hard, really. I'd just have to accept my ephemeral condition and remain passive, like a Madonna by Fra Angelico.

Painting is so strange!

It's like giving thanks.

Like recalling something hidden forever in finitude.

That's right. You get up, trembling, and stand right in the middle of what you don't know, when suddenly you realize that there's *nothing* inside you, or in other words, there's just some silly need to proclaim your love, and it's a love with no object, a love polished to a shine by exile.

Then you have to stop trembling because that tremor is, still, your false personality, and you want to hurry and get down to the child who hasn't yet learned to smooth things over, or learned to let go of the secret lurking within.

Maybe that's all being is: an epiphany of nothing.

The soul searches and, somewhere along the way, graduates from some unrealized maturity to a blind confidence in surrender. Like a spiritual exercise. A cold song sung by a warrior in love with utter defeat.

I'd like all of this to be included in my Annunciation.

That's not asking a lot. Only that the painting paint itself, like life does.

Maybe then, on the canvas, three suns would appear. Wouldn't that be great? Actually, any one of those three suns

would be enough, because its birth—unsolicited, uncalled for—
would radiate a simple and steady light, the kind of light one
would want to see when appearing before God.

There may not be anything else.

There may not be anything other than this absolute
richness where something that I can't see—sacred and
precarious—is always happening.

If I didn't mistrust words, I'd say that this is love or,
really, happiness, not that wad of murky emotions, dripping with
ambition and exhaustion, so often mistaken for it.

I'm talking about being at peace with yourself.

Like the Virgin who looks on and witnesses without
questioning, in profound silence of spirit, the wound that things
inflict when they puncture the circle of our senses. That's all she
asks: not to stain things with the sin of knowledge, to receive
them without the desire to possess them, and even without
astonishment, as the angel descends, from heaven to heaven,
eternally delivering the message of the world.

I just have to wait.

Everything will come from me, is inside me, was always
inside me, though I don't know it yet.

If he had been an architect, Humboldt would have drawn
the plans for an Edenic house, enclosed by a palisade.

For the foundation, he'd have laid a corpse and then,
at ground level, a queen-size bed, complete with two parents,
an ornate hat-rack for hanging a nonexistent hat, a garden with

a swing that would go *trac-trac* whenever the mother opens
the door to call the kids in for lunch. On the left, partly
hidden behind the basement stairs, would sit the booth of the
bureaucrat, someone unseen who talks nonstop and tells you
what *not* to do and, a bit further back, the pulpit of the preacher
(who does the same thing as the bureaucrat, except his speech is
morally infallible, like that of a victim who does nothing more
than attribute to others whatever he can't tolerate in himself).
And also, in the background, barely visible: a bomb shelter,
a place to be alone with your own voice, and a chair for the
architect of the unpredictable, who is totally fed-up and out of
work because the chief architect—Humboldt, that is—refuses
by every means possible to tear down the wall that protects the
house from reality.

"Emma, are you there?"

"Yeah. What's wrong?"

"What if the Humboldt I'm inventing never
actually existed?"

"Well, in a way, he didn't."

"What do you mean?"

"*Your* Humboldt has many facets missing."

"Which ones?"

"You want a list?"

Emma didn't give me time to answer.

"Arrogant but trying to pass for shy, resentful but with
a pretense of nobility, the aggressive type who attacks then take

offense, a liar, mediocre, a psycho, someone, in short, who is totally toxic—need I say more?"

I struggled to stay composed.

I am in Rome, I thought.

In Ro-ma.

Emma was still talking. Now she was attributing false syllogisms to him: "Power is evil. Hell is other people. Ergo, I accuse, and my role is pure." Or, "The revolutionary makes way for the advent of a new society. He does it out of moral superiority. Ergo, I am the revolution."

But I wasn't listening.

I was distracted.

A boy, dragging a toy in one hand, is walking over to me. He has bright blonde hair and light eyes, like the angel Camael.

"*Scusi se la disturbo,*" he says suddenly, "*potrebbe dirmi in quale direzione avanza la primavera?*"

"Oh God, I wish the ground would swallow me up . . . Look who's here."

The Unknown tried to duck out of sight.

"How come you didn't call me earlier," snarled Nobody. "Everything's a mess, I might have been able to help. I'm in no denial about reality."

"*Mon Dieu,*" said The Word House, "it was just a few of us. . ."

"What's he talking about?" Longing asked.

"I don't know, he's nuts."

Nobody, carrying a briefcase, had the air of a lay apostle.

"Could you be just a tad more explicit?" pleaded the Unknown.

"Fine," said Nobody, laying his weapons aside, "but first we have to approve the agenda. I propose we start by analyzing the agro-export bourgeoisie, landowners, neocolonialists, the oligarchy, the dependency, the Port-City, the Instituto Di Tella, the CIA, and Ceferino Namuncurá, which is the vernacular version of the opiate of the masses."

"Ugh," murmured The Word House, "could he be any more of a windbag?"

Longing, who identified with the agenda, asked:

"How long is the meeting going to take? Who's going to pass the information down? Will we get to write evaluations at the end?"

"The most important thing," Nobody continued without deigning to respond, "is to keep our premises clear, namely: 1) The history we were taught is false. 2) Never has an army been able to defeat a people. 3) No social order is suicidal. 4) A people without hate cannot triumph. 5) The best thing children can do with their toys is to break them. 6) The year 2000 will find us either united or dominated. Are we all in agreement thus far?"

"Not one bit," said The Word House, becoming more belligerent. "I object to anachronisms."

"I'd rather talk about Bergman's latest film," stammered the Unknown. "Have you all seen it?"

"Pure nonsense," said Nobody, pounding the table with two hands, the same way someone might delimit a space outside of which there is nothing. "Let me make this perfectly clear: in the revolution, there's no time to intellectualize. And moreover, to build a politics you have to eat, breathe, and sleep politics, you have to give your life over to the project, you can't just jump in unprepared, you have to go through political military training, including boot camp, classes on graffiti, flash protests, blocking bridges with spikes, plus meetings where everyone airs their personal hang-ups, if you catch my drift."

Nobody measured the effect of his words.

Here's the deal: Either we agree on the principle of non-surrender, or they destroy us. You really need to get this through your skulls. At this point, to hand ourselves over alive, even if we hold up brilliantly under torture, is not a victory but a defeat. It's self-annihilation. As a precaution, from now on, all meetings will be armed."

"I have a dentist appointment," Longing suddenly remembered.

"I have an appointment, too, with my chiropractor," added The Word House.

Fear is no dope, The Soul thought.

"Fine," Nobody said, "it's your loss." And he slammed the door as he left, but not before slapping a flyer on the table. It read: "War dispatch. On the date hereof, in observance of the General Order of July 27, 1819, a military squad placed an explosive device outside of the home of Trotta, anti-Peronist professor in the School of Economics at the Universidad de Buenos Aires. This man will henceforth understand that it is not a small matter to ridicule, belittle, and trample on students. Let there be no doubt. Perón Keeps His Promises. Liberation or Dependency. Grow some balls, damn it!"

"And this guy, who the hell does he think he is?"

whispered The Word House. "You'd think he was the *Citoyen Personne . . .*"

"Oh, Emma. What am I saying?"

"Nothing, just bleeding from your wound, that's all."

"You think so?"

"I know so."

After a while, she added:

"Let's see . . . I'll tell you two stories, and you tell me which you like better. In the first, a man walks around watching his own shadow. As he's walking, it occurs to him that maybe the shadow is really him, and that whatever projects the shadow is just an idea, but that idea is false or, worse, useless. In the second story, another man, a mountain-climber this time, walks aimlessly, without fear, without desire. Unlike the first man, he doesn't ask questions because he knows that answers don't exist or, rather, they are indistinguishable from his very being, from his lived experience, and he lives his answers fully, since he doesn't depend on the past or expect anything from the future. You might say he scribbles like a teacher on the blackboard of the sky, except the lines he draws are not words, they're just his life, like an inspired enigma. Your call. Either one would work."

"Work for what?"

"It doesn't matter what. Every time you close your eyes to consider things like this, God goes for a stroll through absolute difference."

I've been happy in Rome, Humboldt. I should get *that* thought into my head. I should appeal to the memory of the dead for guidance. Except why do explosions rumble through the night?

Sometimes I rush out to the street like I'm trying to run away from myself.

Suddenly I'm at the headquarters of the Peronist Youth.

We were together that night. We stood guard to defend the place. In the next room, Tala was talking to his superior. They'd shipped him off to Cuba for two months, and Nana, who he referred to as *my woman*, slept with another guy.

We didn't dare to look at each other. We pretended to pay attention to noises, sirens, dim light filtering through the lattices. By that time, repression was something in plain sight. And nothing so much as stirs in the room where we stand, in silence, stationed at the windows. Only the echo of the voice talking in the next room. Tala's wavering, incredulous voice, and this was the guy who used to harangue thousands of us, who used to inspire us with his iron resolve.

I don't remember a word of that conversation. I'm sure you don't either. Whatever we heard, we probably shouldn't have. We were like kids witnessing a secret, too beautiful or sad.

I've been happy in Rome.

I've accumulated, you might say, experience with improbability.

But what's that moving thing I can't see? Hatred is a failure of imagination, Emma might say. Sadness, a condition, like rain. It will pass.

Rome has seven hills, an angel perched on a round castle, and murky yellow river. I can describe what I see, praise or denigrate it, and it will still be there like a test of something that sharply eludes me.

I have no way out, I said, and geared up for action. This is what fear is like, Emma says, first it paralyzes us, and then it turns us into workaholics.

I decide to lean in and kiss you—a kiss long and drawn-out, like a war. I want it, I say. And, right after that, don't touch me. My body's a hard, transparent house. A crystal vase, you said. Your words shoot into me so deeply, they fly from one obscene extreme to the other, over incredible gestures and the decency I no longer desire (but which still desires me).

I undress, and the piercing scent of your neck. The eternal Madeleine who returns. Her indelible song.

At that instant, Rome vanishes.

Escape itself vanishes, along with the terror of being unable, of not knowing how, to love.

We're made of confusing stuff, Emma said.

This is how I remember you: at the end of a cobblestone street never to be found in Rome. That night, El Tala had his worst run-in yet, because something, for the first time, eluded him. Do you think that's what he thought about at the moment he died? The angel that observes everything from the castle. Giordano Bruno was held prisoner in that castle. I lifted my shirt and showed you my small breasts.

If Emma had copied the scene, she also would have titled it The Annunciation, except that, in this version, the Virgin and the angel would have had the same face, exactly the same.

In the name of the body, you started to pray.

Then I got distracted: How many synonyms does the word enemy have? How many adjectives can qualify it? A strategic enemy, I told myself, isn't the same thing as a temporary enemy, or a class enemy, or an enemy with whom one negotiates from a position of strength. It is not true that a dead enemy is the best enemy. It is *not* true.

I was in an accident once. Something like a beam of light sliced through my life, freezing my insides. But how? Wasn't the crystal vase supposed to be shatterproof? My long hair hung on either side of my face, making my light eyes stand out, and you touched me softly. How disgusting, I thought, all these pigs on the street.

The Peronist Youth, evidently, never left my mind, and somewhere along the way, I left myself behind.

Rome, meanwhile, struck me as ugly, foul, beautiful, depending on the day, hour, season.

There have been so many wars.

Maybe I was wrong, I wanted the wrong thing, I didn't want it enough.

Then I hate myself.

Then Rome burns, along with everything that I myself had been or believed I'd been, leaving behind nothing but the silence of all the living pages, the ones I'll never write.

I am, and always have been, very fortunate, Nobody thought.

Not everyone is born at a time like this, when humanity is in crisis. Crisis pushes us toward commitment, and commitment saves us from a dreary fate.

The old gods, with their old truths, won't cut it anymore. There's plenty of room to invent a world. A world of fantastic and fatal choices: *my* world. I can participate in reality as a subject (not as an object), counteract the venom of power.

Basically, I act like a brat, leave the table, slam the door behind me, and assume my position in battle.

In my solidary heart, love has no limits, neither does hatred.

Both glow on the pyre of a few beautiful books: *The Human Condition, Nausea, The Antichrist, Steppenwolf.*

Nobody is my code name. Changing my name, I invent a *persona*: fiction within fiction. I live in the mask of my desire, in the mask of my experience, prolonging my childhood forever.

For me, faith in revolution is something primordial. I want all or nothing. I'm not interested in mankind as it is now but in how it will be when we take power. I detest the term *acceptance.*

My plan is to live among the poor. And then, to unite with them and with the Organization.

That, in itself, is sensational, the scent of poverty.

Most of all, when this smell mingles with the verbs *to load, to unload, to aim, to fire.*

Every decision determines who I am and, above all, who I will be.

I become something irreproachable, upright, indestructible: the revolutionary, *the highest rung of the human species.*

Like Camus says: What is a rebel? Someone who answers no.

If necessary, I will kill myself to affirm my defiance, my new and terrible freedom.

The Organization takes all of me, it asks everything of me and, by the same token, gives me everything. It requires that, in all circumstances, my actions inform my thoughts, my words produce reality, that I remain consistent with my values, that I enter the struggle with no hope of leaving. In short, that I think like a hero.

It promises me that if I do, things will be clearer, simpler, and cleaner, and that is the truth!

We will develop a new man, a new love, a new truth, a new death. What a fabulous place to live, suspended between worlds! How happy, the end of the rich, of anti-Peronist gunfire, of the quibbling and racketeering bureaucracy. Wonderful that the future looms so near!

Wherever injustice rears its head, I'll be there, to fight. And that way, I'll honor our best men who sowed the fields with their blood . . .

It is my turn to put an end to the *system.* The task is mine—I who will be young forever—and it fills me with energy, intensity, and commitment.

Revolution is a drunken violence, like a first love.

I feel *truly* alive.

One month of my life is fuller than ten years of bourgeois life.

I can feel the warrior in me growing stronger.

I'll cross the line. I'll live out the dream of Death. I'll kill to fight Death. I love the feeling of *transcendence* that comes from that desire.

I'll militarize. Is there any other way to change the face of History? Isn't extolling violence the same thing as extolling life?

I ascend from purity to optimism, beaming with purpose, walled off from anything that could prove me wrong.

I don't stop. I never bend. I make no concessions. I don't feel my anger fade or my confidence falter. I anchor myself to that stubborn little thing that never abandons a good soldier: discipline.

Better a martyr than a traitor.

If I get killed, and I doubt I will, they can say that I lacked understanding but never the desire to desire.

My short, beautiful life will have a purpose.

The important thing, now and forever, is to know *what side* I'm on.

No doubt I'll overcome, thanks to my incredible will for a better nation.

"We did what we had to do," Humboldt says.

"But were we born, or weren't we?"

"You're always running away from yourself."

"I asked you if we were born."

"It depends."

"What do you mean? Depends on what?"

"On you, I guess."

"Do you even understand what happened?"

"Maybe what happened is something beyond description. Or maybe it never actually happened, and the dream we never realized is the key to understanding it. Leave me alone—alright? My left temple is pounding."

"What do you know about the future?"

"I made you suffer, and you'll love me more, a little more, not a lot, in a murkier way. As for me, I slept badly, in short bouts, having restless dreams. There was a blue tint to them, and I was afraid. Someone asked me if I'd ever been loved."

"And then?"

"Then nothing. My fear engulfed us in a cloud, and we mimicked each other's complaints. You grew near-sighted, but it won't be me who will slip off your glasses to kiss you."

"Will I keep writing?"

"Yeah, but your writing will get closer and closer to screaming or silence. Your best line, in my opinion, will be a sentence with no verb, subject, or predicate. A sentence with just one word that is formed from the first letter of other words, whose secret you will want to keep to yourself, and for that reason, it will be incomprehensible, as if you said *nfitsothfteotns*. You never had much patience with the reader's shortcomings. On that point, you'll never budge."

"But, will anything be left of our lives together?"

"Yes. A buried rage that will lash out like a dog when you least expect it. You'll never tolerate lies, injustice, arrogance. Not even the icy good manners of the first world, which you later added to the list of forms of human iniquity and will always strike you as a sophisticated form of cruelty."

"And what about you?"

"I'll be the words that you forget."

The music that corresponds with this scene is "Danse gothique pour la tranquillité de mon âme," by Erik Satie.

"Considering:

"That subversion ferments wherever man, who has to live in freedom under the principles of just reason, becomes corrupt and starts to search for a heaven on earth, letting himself be dominated by his basest and most chaotic passions and appetites;

"That, by subversion we understand, methodologically, that which threatens Order and the sacred interests of the Nation;

"That, when we speak of Order, we do not merely allude to sociopolitical order but to the Natural Order itself, which encompasses what man is and should be;

"That it is easy to imagine the moral depravity, the ideology and even the names of said subversive currents;

"That, among the aberrations associated with that ideology, are atheism, materialism, foreignness, of a Marxist character, and pragmatism, opposed to truth and to all forms of transcendence;

"That the present solution is an exception put in place by the government in the interest of the common good and for the sake of physically eliminating all murderous scum, with the strictest respect for the law, in order to achieve peace and prevent stateless totalitarianism to supplant our flag for a filthy, red rag;

"That these provisions apply equally to the perpetrators, accomplices, and instigating intellectuals who, through their treacherous and indiscriminate crimes, through conspiratorial and underhanded deeds, whether in the shadows or by the light of day, have worked for years in the service of bogus interests to undermine morality and the principles of the Christian faith that define our way of life, and not to exclude the reckless idiots and cannon fodder who might be found anywhere in the National Territory."

Death is bored, death is not.
Is bored, is not.
Is bored, is not.

IV.
Sketch for a
Nocturnal
Annunciation

"What is this?" Emma asks.

"What?"

"This," she says, pointing to a tiny pouch, hardly noticeable, sewn to the inseam of a pant leg.

The Union Lawyer, as if suddenly hit by a stray bullet.

"Cyanide."

"Ah."

The phone rings.

"Don't answer it."

How could she answer it? What could she possibly say that wouldn't sound like a crazy mash of words, like *song McCarthyism dictator son hideout sunshine SUNSHINE*?

"We'll talk later," he says, grabbing his jacket, "I've got a meeting, I'll call you."

The phone keeps ringing, and Emma doesn't take it off the hook.

She remains sitting, utterly blank, with a knot in her chest.

Suddenly she envisions the blue of The Annunciation,

and her heart skips. It's like an outcry that is very old and still only a preamble, a spasmodic surrender, a step toward something that she doesn't yet understand, something that would no doubt be a relief, a surrender that could somehow make way—but for what? Half of her soul is already dead and the other half is dying, I can't paint anymore, she thinks, I'll never paint again—could this blue change the world? Could this man change the world? Sobbing harder and harder, trying not to imagine the horror that starts with a little round pouch, the tiny white night of disgrace stitched into the inseam of a pant leg. Then she decides to leave, and just like that she opens the door, before she even stops crying, and in the stairwell, the monk Athanasius bows to her and, without her noticing, collects her tears into a puddle in his palms where a boat sails with a blue banner that reads *Collegio Romano*, like a god laying out the face of the waters.

I wish I hadn't told you, Humboldt, I hate to worry you, but El Bose has been coming at me from all sides. I run into him at the movies, on the banks of the Tiber, when I was getting an ice-cream the other day, and last night, in my own room. Not that I'm scared of him, it's not that. How could I be scared of El Bose? Though sometimes I feel like I might drown in his eyes, like they're so far on the other side of time that I can't remember who I used to be or, even worse, who I want to be, if I still want anything at all . . . He sat on my bed and, with no preamble whatsoever, told me how Sonia had called him to account: "For guys who come off as revolutionaries, you're a bunch of dinosaurs when it comes to girls, you're all stuck in the stone ages, not one bit more progressive than my grandfather."

Clearly her words affected him. But that isn't what I came here to tell you, he said. I came here to tell you when, how, and why I quit political work.

He said that he'd announced at a meeting of cadres that he didn't want any more trouble. Apparently he had long stopped believing in the happiness of revolution, he didn't even know who he was any more in the middle of that asphyxiating mess, he asked himself how he might go back to living a normal life, which might involve going out for pizza in Banchero, taking a leisurely walk, sleeping, possessing something other than secrets, dealing with regular problems like anyone else. He went on for hours, Humboldt, he was obviously upset, as if suffering in some deep dark corner of his soul. He had asked them—though his questions fell on deaf ears—about the line between loyalty and betrayal, between principles and opportunism, between criticism and a lack of accountability to victims. He wanted to know whether a person could maintain a degree of skepticism without losing the will to act, and whether it was possible to scrutinize the failures of the huge resistance operation we'd undertaken.

He told me that he'd called a meeting to discuss it. He proposed a political debate to evaluate all the different proposals that had emerged among organization leaders. Not everyone was on the same page, he said. Some people justified the use of force without question, like they belonged to the Perreté in the ultra-left, where internal debate was practically unheard-of. Those guys just kept quiet, as if biding their time until conflicts escalated. But some people, he said, and particularly right now, objected to that approach, though not on principle—because we all know perfectly well, he said, that you can't be a revolutionary without using violence to exert a counterforce equal to or greater than what, these days, is exercised by the State. No, their objection was that the counterforce had to be formed collectively within the Movement, and that wasn't happening, not by a long shot. Instead, the exact opposite was true, the use of force was a step taken by the leadership alone, without mass support. And according to El Bose, the leaders sanctioned him right then and there.

Clearly, they told him, he didn't understand or didn't choose to understand that we were already at war, and that lack of understanding was ample evidence of his ideological shortcomings. But which war, he'd asked them. The war you're referring to is the war that *they* want. It has nothing whatsoever to do with anything we proposed. He told them that it was insane to go underground in the name of the Movement. Many of the violent attacks at the time struck him as madness, though frankly, there came a point when he could barely distinguish what was crazy from what wasn't—every day brought a new catastrophe, someone else detained, gone missing, committing suicide, like our friend in law school who threw himself off the balcony of the courthouse, and no one could say a thing, they just brushed everything under the rug. If this continues, the leaders of the organization will be mounting a military pantomime in a vacuum. But they blew him off, he said. It's been a while since they've discussed anything of substance, and this meeting was no exception.

El Bose looked pale, I can't do this anymore, he told them, since when do we talk about things in terms of win or lose, as far as I know it was never a matter of winning or losing, at least not for me it wasn't, and the truth is, the word *win*, at this point, sounds the same as the word *die*.

He said things like that, which the leadership rejected, deciding instead to lock him up for a week so that they could *reexamine* his ideas.

And guess who the jailer was?

Me, Humboldt, and none other. I, who spent my life condemning people who push their views onto others. *I* locked him up for dissent.

And, what's worse, I don't remember any of it: not the apartment where we supposedly lived, not the documents we discussed, not even what we did at night, in the afternoon, in the morning, when occasionally, I suppose, we would have detected our confusion and fear.

It almost felt as if I were listening to Emma: "What a genius, El Bose! He flashed you the friendly face of National Interest."

I swear I didn't dream it.

Sitting right here, perfectly calm, almost amused at times, he told me all about it.

Afterwards I asked him, "And what about me, what was I doing?"

"Nothing, you reminded me that the Montoneros were the armed branch of the Peronist movement, that one military action is worth more than eighty I-don't-know-whats put together, that I shouldn't forget the dead, that it was never a question of just lying on our backs for Perón, that we won't be taken advantage of just like that, and all about the Movement's shortcomings and the rise of the bureaucracy and the cadre party, and so forth, that whole convoluted mess, all day, nonstop, until all hours, you were really on a tirade, you wouldn't let up."

"And did I convince you?"

"Sure, and hell froze over."

"Did we at least get along?"

"More or less, you had zero sense of humor, same as Humboldt, you guys were really two of a kind."

And then he grew quiet, as if to give me time to respond. But the words died in my mouth, Humboldt, one after the other. An endless list of questions arose and fell away, and nothing left my lips. Like some desire, clumsy, absolute. My body and its awkwardness, my body and its amputated memory.

Forgetting is active.

"Sorry to interrupt," said The Unknown, "I'd like you to meet two people who are interested in joining up."

The Wasp and The Will said hello.

"Who are they, the Dynamic Duo?" thought Nobody irritably.

"We're in the middle of a meeting," he informed them, "but sit down. We're busy tonight, we have some work to do on a cop."

"Wait, what's going on here?" The Word House complained. "He recruited them to work at the Student Center, not at Popular Army Headquarters."

"Yeah," said The Unknown, "she has a point, this is a serious screw-up. Besides, since when do we do political work on these premises? These guys aren't ready to be here."

"This discussion isn't open to the public," said Nobody. "But on the other hand, they might as well hear it. A revolution where no one gets killed isn't a revolution."

At that moment, a blind man entered the café selling stickers with the phrase *Smile, The Warlock loves you*.

The Word House clutched her head.

"This country is driving me up a wall. Our Old Man is never going to die, The Warlock is never going to die, the military are never going to die. This stuff doesn't happen anywhere else. Why do we constitute such a fucking exception?"

"Excuse me," she said, "but as far as I know, the labor class organization..."

"Working class, working," Nobody corrected.

". . . is worried about more than having good aim, damn it."

"And you, what do you make of all this?"

The Soul had spoken in a hushed voice, directing her words to Longing, who was nibbling a Jorgito snack cake.

"That we all have bad manners."

"And what's so wrong with that? You don't like vulgarity or something?"

"No, my parents taught me not to use bad words."

"This week I made thirty signs, distributed 100 flyers, and pamphleteered twice in the Bidart Campos lecture hall at the law school," said The Will, tucking her hair behind her ears. "I am Assistant Professor of Theory of Law." She was sporting a Ban-Lon cardigan.

"And where did you find *her*? Just started, and she already wants a promotion," thought Nobody. "But she doesn't represent the masses, she doesn't even represent her own grandma."

The Wasp, on the other hand, spoke little. He would

have rather been studying the Civil Code. His favorite chapters were "Of Persons of Visible Existence," "Of Missing Persons Under Presumption of Death," "Of Acts Produced by Force, Fraud and Fear," "Of Redhibitory Vices," "Of Confusion," "Of the Manner of Computing Intervals of Time in the Law," and "Of the Extinction of Servitudes."

"Guerilla activity is a common offense," Perón was saying on the TV. "We are Justicialistas. As for those who allege the unconfessable, those foolish enough to believe they can co-opt our Movement. . ."

"Is he trying to tell us something?" the Unknown asked uneasily.

"He's just railing against the tired Right and the sepoy Left," Nobody assured him.

"And what about us, what are we?"

"Neither the victors nor the vanquished. . . at least for now," the blind man with the stickers interjected. "So how about that Kempes? Was that a goal, or what?"

"You know what, sweetie? I'm out of here," said The Word House.

"Aren't you going to that rally in William Morris?" asked Longing.

"What are you talking about? That was in 1972."

Perón was still running his mouth.

"To our concealed enemies, to those who traitorously work from inside and with the backing of foreign funds..."

The Soul couldn't believe it.

He just called us mercenaries! I'd much rather live, she thought, between a star and two swallows.

Oh kid, thought El Bose, you still don't know the half of it . . . I'm not sure if you remember, but by the time I dropped out, the shit had really hit the fan. Mostly on fronts like ours, the student sympathizers, the ones who joined when everything was still all fun and games, they started to have their own ideas about things, there was no organized pull-out, it was everyone man for himself, and they started dropping like flies, running around in circles with no fucking clue, basically, the classic escape scenario, because everyone knew deep down that we were walled in and that, this time, the wall was real. Let's just say that, until Rucci, we hadn't cut ties with our Old Man, not completely anyway. It was a big deal, I remember thinking 'this is the beginning of the end,' and it was, literally, because that was when our guys started to talk, even that one chief turned into a snitch, remember that? He was a real heavyweight, too, up to his neck in the project, but he ratted out who knows how many people, like any other informant, some spy, some CIA agent, he even handed over centers of operations, and sure enough, the ambushes started, raids, a whole string of killings, and that's when it hit me, we hadn't even seen the worst of it, what we'd seen up to that point was nothing. And that's when I realized it was all over, from now on it's going to be...but hey, why the hell am I telling you this? You know it by heart. I'd better shut my mouth or pretty soon I'll start reading you the CVs of the survivors who went on to become judges, doctors, diplomats, tango dancers, that kind of bullshit.

Dear Longing, little mermaid,

I've hardly written a word for months, it's awful, not one measly prose poem (my new name for my borrowed bits of prose). Instead I've been spending my days working on a vernacular rendition of *Out of the Past*. Did I ever tell you, I adore film noir? The crimes of passion, the linguistic sparring between the detective and the blonde. What I love the most is the atmosphere, so urban and gloomy that one feels quite at home. Tell me, what do you think of this premise: a man, who turns out to be a serial killer, goes after a group of orphans. They're little misfits, the kind who go hunting for frogs in public parks. And since they're Marxist Leninists, they're not afraid of the bogeyman that frightens all the naughty kids who don't finish their porridge. Soon, they begin to organize, they change their names, their schools, their soccer teams, where they go to summer camp, and they start shooting their slingshots while hollering *woo-hoo! We almost shot his eye out!* And the man goes to every length to defend himself, with tanks, machine guns, helicopters, until reinforcements arrive and there's a raid in the playground, and screams, threats, vulgarities ring out over the loudspeakers, and as soon as everything is broken, smashed to utter shit, one of the neighbors utters the words *The house is in order.* And in a reverse-angle shot, you see the frogs, who turn out to be blondes, femme fatales, cold and beautiful, floating like corpses in the murky puddles. And the little misfits, you ask? *Disparus* forever, in the fade-out. on the screen. Too simplistic, maybe? Someone told me that it sounds like Fritz Lang, crossed with Bresson.

Don't believe it, little mermaid, it's not easy to put up with the emptiness of the multicultural colony, not even for me, and my extravagance knows no bounds. But I don't want to die in a foreign country. If I had the chance, I'd travel clear across the world, but I'd hurry right back. I prefer inefficiency to success, a cigarette to any sort of work ethic, destitution to the Protestant ideal of four dogs, four televisions, four cars, four egos, et cetera.

I tell myself to wait. Some form of inspiration will come.

Form, according to Adorno, is the past sedimented, and in me, things didn't sediment at all. I don't know what will happen after more time passes. All I can say is that life is my new plaything: I go to parties, fall in love, jump with admirable dexterity across the terrain of a dissembling soul.

And what about you? Are you well? Have you begun to figure out that there is no such thing as *the* woman because the woman—not all of her—simply *is?*

I hope you remain in high demand, and that love makes you feel like a light that travels the world with a pink polka-dot umbrella.

We all miss you here, even the people who don't know you personally love you very much, and the situationists, and the giraffes at the zoo, too.

I send you a cryptic kiss.

Smooch!

Your Emperor Très Noir.

P.S. *Peccato* that Argentina will never have its own Veronica Lake.

"That was a terrible night for Emma," Athanasius, next to me, sighed.

I noticed his worn-out suit and bird-like gaze alighting on the steps to the Church of Gesu. Evidently this man appeared at my side and disappeared purely on whim, and it didn't entirely bother me.

"Here Ignacio de Loyola wrote his famous *Exercises*, inspired by the teachings of Ludolf of Saxony," he added as if I had actually requested the information. "Ignacio was a soldier of religion and an athlete of severity, which is to say a poet of war who instituted, after a fashion, a monopoly of images to communicate directly with God. Like any voluntary mystic, he was driven by a fervor for obedience."

I let my weight rest against the gate.

The Roman night, too, I thought, with its piazzas and cast iron street lamps, the rumor of its river, and its cornices adorned with sculptures, is arbitrary and capricious and in the end improbable. I can't go on.

The monk confined himself to waiting.

"A terrible night," he repeated. "One of those nights when the world slips away from us completely, like now. In a sense, nothing happened (what's important always lacks a plot). Or, to put it another way, something happened that had happened before: as if a flying arrow had suddenly caught up with her, Emma came to a halt. Her eyes were swollen from all the crying, and her body was frozen stiff, but that didn't prevent her from being shocked. She was standing at precisely the right angle of a triangle whose base coincided with her childhood home and whose sides with the reverberations of that *same* house in future memory. Then she thought: why does pain always swing us back to the beginning of the beginning? The question hit her like a whip, and she couldn't hold back her thoughts any longer. What if I painted for that reason? To become that little girl, the girl who always knew that the blue in our vision coincides precisely with its own absence. As if the terrible were a kind of harmony—and God an idea we have no words for, which is to say, in absolute terms, no idea. And, at that very instant, the wind nudged the boats of some fisherman to shore (it doesn't matter which boats they were, or where they were headed)."

I looked at him uncomprehending.

"Ah, Emma," Athanasius sighed, as if Emma were with us. "In the night of reason, delirium edges on epiphany, destruction on salvation."

The old man's tone grew magisterial, as if he'd completely forgotten about me and now spoke only for his own benefit, or for absolute time.

"The infinite labyrinth of the soul is called, on that hazy night, The City of Voluptuous Truth or The Book of the Vacant Throne, which are the same, because nothing is anything more than the same. I die of not dying, the soul says, and then, it forms the ossature of consciousness, so it may hide in that most tentative place from which all things emanate."

Yeah, he forgot all about me.

"This has been known for centuries by adherents of the expansive School of Reverie and The Finite. For them, *c'est la matière qui imagine le ciel.* You have to encircle the beloved (dreamed, departed, lost) object, contour it, and let yourself be thwarted, thrown off, until you come to nothing nothing nothing, forever and forever. An absurd ballet, it seeks neither *this* nor *that*. God is that interval. The buried trace that announces, fatally, the world."

"And this," he added after a while, as if waking from a dream, "Emma didn't realize. Just as she didn't realize that she painted in order to embody, in herself, a reality . . . Nevertheless, I spotted her one day standing mute before a painting by Ludovico Cardi. I myself have looked at that painting in that way. I have seen its moon, which isn't quite a circle with no macula but more of a sphere that appears gnawed, abrasive, riddled with craters, and then I asked myself things that left me trembling, for example: is it possible to explain what is on the sole basis of what isn't, of what will never be, or even, of what could never be?

A similar thought had been forming in Emma, though later, in her sketchbook, she censored her own feelings, copying down the formula: *To reconstruct the empirical reality on the basis of the ideal reality.*

Obviously, Cardi intimidated her. For that reason, whenever she copied an Annunciation, she liked to honor the concentric arrangement of its elements. That is natural. Giotto, too, drawing with no compass, inserted circles wherever they would fit, ordered vertically, the high and the low, the celestial and the earthly. The primacy of the circle, moreover, comes from Plato, and Emma was fascinated by aporias.

In other words, Emma held true to her hypotheses: she picked the simplest figures (the most perfect) and arranged them in a composition that rotated around a center, forcing them to rotate around it too, just as consciousness supposedly orbits around truth. That is how, in all her fervor, she failed to recognize that what she painted was none other than a precise likeness of a nonexistence."

The little old man winced, as if someone had accused him of something.

"Don't assume, Miss, that I didn't try on several occasions to disabuse her of her error. But of course, it was a thankless task. It isn't easy to bring someone closer to an intuition about appearances, where the stone is covered with wounds. Vertigo, the worm of subject matter, misleading ellipsis, and all offences to scansion begin by penetrating form, and they end up reducing everything to the emotional effect of seeing night erupt inside night."

Athanasius scratched his head.

"No, it wasn't easy. Especially with autumn weighing down that cemetery-city . . . In Rome, on the other hand, it is easier to find the puppet theaters, which are great human dreams."

There were long pauses between his sentences, and I had to move in closer to hear.

"Nonetheless, I often challenged her to look more closely, and to stop aspiring for perfection. I knew this was the only way to open her mind and heart to new possibilities, perspectives, phobias, doubts, ruptures, proliferation, energy. In short, she might discover, in the impossibility of order, the inflammatory joy of freedom that would prepare her to face death . . . Day and night, I dreamed of the painting Emma would produce once she understood that all presence is, in essence, a fantasy of absence. I envisioned that canvas in its disturbed splendor, its sullen beauty. There, every gesture was amplified, the curves were broken, unbalanced, as in that open, repetitive web stretching between redundancy and entropy which is the space of travel, I'm referring to life. That painting

would be called Nocturnal Annunciation, and I would have it
in my Museum. It would mark a narrow victory (but a victory
nonetheless) over the incomprehensible, because Death would be
represented there in the absence of representation, opening the
door to a blind reconciliation between desolation and everything
that, without being, is."

The little old man looked at me, suddenly, with mad
delight.

"My dream came true, Miss. That night, when she finally
managed to return to the apartment on la calle Uruguay, Emma
did something unprecedented: on the Annunciation on the table,
she spontaneously scribbled some words and, beside them, their
definitions:

—world: your mouth
—time: stars over a garden terrace and the dawn that erases them
one by one
—tenderness: the take-over of The Winter Palace
—heart: the day after tomorrow on the banks of a river
—blue: nothing is everything and vice versa

Of course she went to bed thinking that she'd ruined that
Annunciation.

She still didn't realize that, in art, there is no vision
without blindness.

"I'm so excited, sweetie, I met a new guy in the Lit department."

"Yeah? What's he like?" Longing asked.

"He's a stud. I practically fainted when I saw him."

"Is he one of us?"

"No, but he's amenable."

"Better than un-amenable. How did you meet him?"

"I just walked over and hit on him."

"Isn't that hard?"

"What, to hit on a guy? There's nothing to it. You just cross your legs, give him a look, and act like a ditz."

I'm hopeless, Longing thought.

"He's got a friend who isn't bad, you want me to introduce you?"

"No, I'm too busy with the hostile differences between Perón and the People's camp."

Longing looked like she was concentrating. But a moment later, she asked again:

"And, have you guys . . .?"

"No, so far we've just made out. And we talk a lot. Well, he does most of the talking."

"What does he talk about?"

"I don't remember."

"And what do you do?"

"Nothing, I just let him talk, and then I interrupt him with the Roca-Runciman Treaty. Now I'm lecturing him on the Uturuncos."

"Did you explain the *Populorum Progressio*, the politico-technical teams, the US invasions of Santo Domingo, the Peronist Youth reaching across the country?

"You want him to spray me with a can of Raid?"

"Why would he spray you with Raid?"

"Those topics aren't very *érotiques*."

At that, Nobody walked in carrying a briefcase.

"What time is it?" the two asked him in unison.

"Don't talk to me. I just went undercover."

On the television in the café, a stone-faced Isabelita: "Let there be no doubt, the Armed Forces, ever more aware of their institutional responsibility . . ." At her side, equally unmoved, The Warlock, The Retired First Corporal, The Next In Line, The Amanuensis, The Secretary, Portable Memory, The Gatekeeper, and The Ex-Lightning Rod of all evils sent against General Perón's health.

"What a charade," said Longing.

"Charade, my ass, *chérie*. At the very least, the strategy of the enemy has changed. And at most . . . we're losing, like in *la guerre*."

At that moment, an official stepped forward and spoke to a soldier:

"Subordinate," he said, "you are not alone. Keep moving forward, even if you lose heart. Everything is within the law. Everything is outside the law, as well. Your war is clean. Your objective: one death every five hours. Focus on efficacy, method. Your service record will be impeccable: not a single one of them should get out alive."

The Soul sighed in her corner.

"Oh," she said, "it's all so complicated! And on top of everything, Nobody wants me to memorize all the anniversaries."

"All the what?"

"The anniversaries. You know, days when you celebrate something?"

"I remember one," The Word House became animated, "the 29th of June!"

"What do we celebrate on June 29th?"

"The ingenious theory absolving Perón of responsibility."

Longing surreptitiously pointed to the TV.

On the screen, live and direct, were the Navy, Army, and Air Force. And behind them, various representatives from the Legitimate Military Wing, the Joint Chiefs of Staff, including the Moderate Wing, the generals, cavalry arms, cabinet ministers, multinational executives, members of the Episcopate, unionists, ambassadors, all the chiefs of the garrisons, brigades, units, tactical commands, torture facilities, and other defenders of national disgrace, all in uniform and advancing like locomotives.

"Make no mistake," said Prince Videla of the Little Mustaches, "the guerilla attacks are not targeted at entrepreneurs, or at labor leaders, or at the military, but at the Country as a Whole."

The Country as a Whole gave a quick bow and greeted the camera: "I am not a Liberated Vietnam, nor do I wish to be, God saves and protects me, there is nothing quite like my Grand Ol' Blue and White."

At that very moment, The Will burst in.

"Come on, don't waste time on this foolishness. What was it that General Giap always said about the rifle? I need it for a flyer I'm making."

Writing, Humboldt, is like plenitude. You look in one direction, and nothing. You look in the other direction, nothing again. All that effort just to sit, in the end, covered in the crumbs of nothingness.

Right now, for example, with everything laid to record on this page, you abandon me, and so it's as if every line, every word, were a grand farewell, a terrible ceremony marking, at the very most, that someone was here, except I don't know who that someone was, I don't even know when he disappeared, or where he went.

How can I explain it? By writing, you decorate pain. You lay out plants, photographs, tablecloths, and then stay on to live there peacefully, relying on the notion that nothing can get any worse because, in reality, if something already hurts a lot, how could it hurt more?

It's like having nothing to fear because you're already afraid.

You believe in what you wrote, and one day, you say, with a straight face: This is my life. I built this fortress and locked myself inside, and now, I'm nothing more than my steps on the staircase and the parapets and the crypts and the cracks throughout this starry place, so haunted by the palpable presences that I dreamed up in order to frighten myself (you were one of my ghosts).

Everything is so painfully real, Humboldt. But what good is any of it? Before you know it, you'll have to

say 'Goodbye, things! I don't need an umbrella anymore,
I won't move anyone else to compassion with the little
nocturnal music that was, perhaps, the very night in me,
like a station for workers.'

I miss your warmth in the bed. No, I'll never
replace you with a hot water bottle.

You'd never guess what I did today.

I bought myself a blue dress, skin-tight, strapless,
on the Via del Panico.

The shop girl said: "Trees blossom at the end of
winter, and now you'll blossom too, this fits you perfectly,
but don't forget to blossom."

That's when I thought: What if actually I hated
him?

It's important to have someone to hate, you
taught me that. I'll have to make an effort. I don't even
know how to begin. Anyway, I tell myself, it's bound to
be better than things right now. But what are *things right
now?* Things right now consist of being tied together for
all eternity, pretending to ignore what we very well know.
For example: inside what you call *us*, there was another
inside, which I never entered. Years spent erecting your
walls, and suddenly everything rotted. Even your chest
began to swell like a shield for covering the lives of others.
I never really liked the shape of your chest, Humboldt.
Who could have known that with you, of all people, I
needed a lie detector.

I know what you're going to say: You have
a poison tongue, you're nuts, what happened never
happened, I love you like crazy.

Oh, Humboldt, fear makes you, like me, talk nonsense.

The other day I woke up from a dream with the word *bat* stuck in my head. I don't know why, but I thought about those goals at the 1978 World Cup. People with bongos, flags, trucks speeding down la avenida Pavón.

Can you play soccer in a blood-soaked country?

Can you shout *gooooal* as if giving the killers a round of applause?

The people are never in the wrong, we used to say. That same old story about the poor stealing parquet and burning it to grill their meat, our Old Man riding around on motorcycles with teenage girls from the Secondary Student Union—that's just typical anti-Peronist crap. Long live Perón, damn it!

But I witnessed that with my own two eyes.

Nobody remembered the Garage Olimpo torture center, much less your body.

It's terrible to live while playing dead.

Right now, adrift in Rome, I sail up the dirty yellow Tiber and head nowhere. I've managed to flawlessly simulate a shipwreck. I'm leaving behind all the bridges, motorcycles, and thoughts that someone, maybe, thought for me. And that, and Rome, and the great Italian *notte* are the only things I'll ever receive in the doling out of symbolic goods.

I've lost my name. I've lost all my names. After desperation, after massacre, all that remains for me is the curl of certain letters, an inconsolable wonder. Not wisdom. Not salvation. Maybe just a desert with no history where nothing stands for nothing. Something like that.

The questions never stop coming. Weren't we fighting for a just cause? Didn't we want a less imprisoning world? How come I saved myself, when you didn't? Did I really save myself, or am I just a corpse talking to herself on the street, retching up stuff that doesn't matter to anyone? Did I ever experience pleasure? For that reason, did I take up arms as if dedicating an obscene book to a lonely, destitute creature—me? Is not having a future a good thing? Will I still be alive on March 11, 2033?

I should really keep hating. Hatred *that isn't tinged by desire.*

I have to see you, little by little, by the light of every one of your faces. Maybe that would cure me of your monumental desertion of my body.

Today is Sunday. It's raining. In 15 minutes, I will answer the phone.

It's so refreshing to write trivial things!

Alright, El Bose said, you just focus on my green shirt and suntan, and I'll do the talking. I'll ask you the tough questions, the ones you never dare to ask, I'll ask them to you, just like when I handed your little notebook, don't be scared, they're part of the gift.

What's the relationship, for example, between politics and crime?

In what ways does a pursuer of the absolute

resemble a fanatic?

How did we start to resemble prisoners kneeling in a cell of our own design?

Remember, you can't talk. We're no longer in that apartment where I had to sit and listen to you for hours.

I'm not being *questioned*. Nobody gives me orders. I don't have to get upset, or feel like a fool, or say you know what I could give a shit about your orders so fuck off.

I'm saying that, in politics, when you aspire to purity, when you chase after perfection, you always land in unreality. Also, sectarianism derives from impotence.

I say this like a night superimposed on a night.

I'm showing it to you like a movie. We, the rebellious kids, all cut from the same idealist cloth. So we're interchangeable. We enlist in order to immerse ourselves all the faster in the whirlwind of violence and death.

How the hell did that happen?

One day our guys started dropping like flies, some started talking, they just went to pieces like the rich kids from Suipacha and Juncal. The hell with awareness and understanding of the project. We had to act fast, the enemy was breathing down our necks. So we concentrated on what we *could* control: ourselves. We had to attack individualism. We had to weed out, once and for all, anything that could weaken our will to fight, and we started with the obstacle of ourselves, our trivial personal lives. We were at the far end of some kind of anomalous logic, caught up in preachy, moralistic, hermetic tough guy talk: in sum, politics stepped up to another level—and so did reality. We started to brush over our disagreements, without suspecting, or maybe *because* we suspected, that finding the truth is hard work, it's complex and slippery, it rarely comes wrapped in cellophane with a pretty bow.

With the crisis came the ideologue, who was also tough, hard-working, practically ascetic. By his account, smug and narcissistic, the war we'd embarked on was a sublime pact that couldn't be broken by petty emotions. We kept hiding behind our jargon, our closed ranks, our ruthless self-criticism, with no thought to safety, our own or anyone else's—this, combined with a lethal embrace of armed struggle as a test of our courage and commitment. Every act of force would serve, we said, to gather strength, that's the way to iron out contradictions. Where was our strategy to build a national front, our commitment to the neighborhoods, the very thing that differentiated us from the ultra-left? Didn't we agree not to break from our grass-roots? After a while, even our aliases stopped working for us. We had to come up with new ones, hide even better from ourselves. Some guys managed to bring something of themselves to their new name: a favorite pipe, a need to please, a lack of body-awareness, a simple faith in the world, allergies, stuff like that. Suddenly it was a matter of surviving. One day at a time. We ran ourselves ragged escaping from one house to another, not even having time to count how many people we lost from our own ranks (not to mention the masses, who were slipping from our grasp). Exiles in our own country, unable to contact our families, we embraced duplicity, a secret identity, in order to travel under the radar, blend in and disappear like fish in the sea. Our behavior had a peculiar character, by the way, in the shadows.

I'm going to stop here.

You already know the rest, it's all summarized in the eternal garbage dump massacre, doomed to keep repeating, although the names and dates change.

You can go back to your business now, kiddo, pardon the interruption. I'd only wanted the little book to contain everything, including our own responsibility.

"What do you think of what I'm saying, Humboldt?"

"That you always were, and always will be, your own lead character. Leave me in peace, will you?"

"Why are you talking to me like this?"

"I don't know, your reactionary attitude is kind of pissing me off."

"What do you mean?"

"Don't act like an angel all of a sudden, you're not very convincing. Why don't you tell the story of how they searched for me in Quilmes and, when I wasn't there, they tore everything to shit, broke the radiators apart, set clothes on fire, trampled all the dinnerware, broke closets, smashed tables, all the while shouting like possessed maniacs, taking out their rage on whatever happened to be at hand, hollering and swearing that they were going to rip me to shreds."

"I forgot."

"Yeah, and you also forgot that I took the 22

downtown, that I was spared from military service by being the only son of a widowed mother, that I had tuberculosis as a kid, that my family was so poor that every summer my sister and I sucked on ice like it was ice-cream."

"Don't exaggerate, and stop making things up, quit trying to make me feel sorry for you. I need to find my own role, and my own non-role, if I even want to go on living. Only then will I be able to look, as Baudelaire suggested, at my body and my heart without disgust. Who could ever calculate the orbit of his desire? It's impossible to know where we're headed. One day walking on the via del Corso, I saw a sky go white with swallows. I burst out laughing like a lunatic. Spring had arrived, and I didn't know where you were, at what hour of what world."

"Calm down, you're hysterical."

"And you, stop lying to me."

"I'm not lying."

"Were we happy at least?"

"We made the enemy tremble, so we must have done *something*."

"I asked you if we were happy."

"If you're referring to our *sentimental education*, it was difficult, beautiful, and mostly to my credit. And for that reason, I had the right to say *I'm abandoning my own creation*. And that's just what I did."

"Our love was a war then?"

"Bingo."

"Can't you be more specific though? The day, the hour, the pronouns, the beds. I want to know who you were, what kind of truth is locked inside the questions I can't ask."

"It was nobody's fault."

"Yes or no, before or after, be exact."

"I thought. You said. There was pleasure. Pain. My issues."

"So the body is the origin of everything?"

"Sad man in your shadow. That time that. You or nothing. How nice it feels to be alone."

"Traitor! Scumbag! Master of disguises!"

The music that corresponds to this scene is *Story*, by John Cage.

Humboldt thought: Thirteen, fourteen, up to fifteen hours a day my old man labored, he was a metal worker, I earned more than him, when high school was over I worked in a cooperative for a while, after that I started to study, my old man had gotten it into his head that I should end up doing this or that, so I wouldn't have to struggle like he did, taking rotating shifts, sleeping in the daytime, not even resting on weekends, and that gave birth to a kind of pride, that I was at The University, he had hopes for me, you could see that from a mile away, even when, when I was little, he took me with him to pick up his paycheck, and we stopped at a bar and he told all his friends this kid's got what it takes, he's going to make it, you'll see, despite my shame, despite the hatred I felt when I played ball in the vacant lot and just across the fence, the blonde students from St. Georges stood like proof of everything out of my reach. He was in the production sector, my old man, which had the most dangerous conditions, it was a noxious place, and his hours were too brutal for anyone to withstand, I didn't really know what that place was about, from the outside it looked monstrous, a hulking, filthy thing that spat out smoke, spewed pestilent slime at the banks of the Riachuelo, in my house they didn't talk much about the factory, just that same story of getting up when it was still dark and hopping the bus that passed by Mitre and then the stop in front of the iron fence and punching his card and heading through a long sort of passageway, windowless, with two skylights and the tremendous stench of solvent, where my old man, according to him, awaited his coworkers. The men didn't talk, they never exchanged a word, they smoked their cigarettes and then filed off to the areas with extremely high levels of toxicity from the substances used, all of them carcinogenic, and you could see them looking down, faces drawn, resigned, my old man the same as any other, until that day when they found a lump in his back and he died shortly after, I was eighteen, and after that things get fuzzy, what I know I only know because they told me, to be perfectly honest, I hardly ever saw him, when I got home from school, if he wasn't at the factory, he was sleeping, I know that he drank, that he looked down when he walked, and that people liked his sense of humor, which was a little dry, that's all I know. I know nothing else.

"You're going to need to write a report."

"What about?"

"About what we discussed at the meeting."

"But nobody was paying any attention to you."

"All the more reason. So the record shows that
I did everything I could. That I told them about Triacca,
monopolies, import substitution, the local leaders,
the Supreme Council of the Justicialistas, the fascists
ensconced in the General Confederation of Labor, and all
the others enmeshed in the State's ideological apparatus.
And also about the nation of metalworkers versus the
liberated socialist nation, and about the characterization
of the moment and the strategic objectives, and about the
vanguard party, the organic intellectual and the construction
of socialism. All that, and nothing. As if they were all
listening to the rain. Revolutionary training isn't possible
if people can't even attend to the priorities of the moment.
Write!"

"Should I include that bum from the Movement for
Socialism and his nasty lies?"

"Include everything."

"What about your thoughts on the firing range and
starting military training?"

"Yeah, yeah, all of it. And sign it with: *To strike so
that one day peaceful negotiation might be possible, History stops
for no one, Perón returns, Happy Socialist Homeland.* Don't
forget that it's October 17th."

"I don't know what's happening to me," said Longing, "I'm having some kind of existential block, I don't know what to do."

"Let's see," mused The Word House, who was wearing a stethoscope around her neck, "I'm going to administer a General Knowledge Test, maybe that will help. Of the 223 endnotes in Kepler's *Somnium*, which refers to the emotional geography of the soul?"

"Number 542."

"Co-rrect. And what is life like in the Torrid Zone of the sub-volcanoes, taking into account that the ground is porous and perforated with grottos?"

"Wondrous. Individuals are born and die on the same day, but not without first having lived one never-ending, unforgettable night. Entire generations die out every day, with the consolation of having known what it is to be a wanderer."

"In my opinion, having no place to call home doesn't seem so swell," said The Word House taking offense.

"That depends. Plutarch, in his famous dialogue "On the Face of the Moon," says that, on that one night, men become children again."

"Did somebody call me?" The Unknown asked.

Now we're in trouble, thought The Word House. Apparently we haven't already had enough metaphysics, medicine, and astronomy of the passions.

"Don't change the subject," Longing pleaded. "I

need to know what's going on with me, why I can't write. Maybe it's because I don't love enough? Or I don't suffer enough? Or I don't spend enough time in silence?"

"I don't have the faintest idea, kiddo."

At that, The Unknown offered his (unwanted) opinion.

"Poetry is just a matter of living. At night you might think: the musical ear of Death, sexually ripe, writes a letter to a man who has been pedaling his bicycle for years, for no reason whatsoever, along a path lined with cherry trees when, from the left, a drowsy young lady appears carrying a blue umbrella with pink polka dots, but that's another story."

"What does the letter say?" Longing asked with sudden interest.

"You are alone. Few gestures are possible. Happiness cannot be sought."

"Does the man read it?"

"Yes."

"And what does he do?"

"Nothing, he just keeps pedaling."

"Is that all?"

"No, that's not all. The bicycle goes and, as it does, it produces a sweet sadness, which does not hinder the explosion of desire or the small crimes inside delicate flowers."

"I don't like it," remarked The Word House, "it seems like a story hatched by a psychopath."

At that instant, The Soul appeared.

"I stopped by so that you could measure my

shadow," she said simply.

The Soul was a hidden sympathy, she dreamed about the waxing face of the Moon when Saturn, according to Galileo's *Conversation with the Starry Messenger*, aligns with equinoctial axis of Earth and is reflected in the Pleiades constellation.

Death, who was secretly observing all of this, held her ears.

She wore a red dress.

My time to come alive is growing near, she thought.

Maybe this March…

V.
1976

In another one of my versions, Humboldt, we sunk into a sexual morass. I thought of nothing else. I forgot to study prosopopoeia, hypallage, the rhetorical construct of the I, even to read beautiful books. Then one day, you slammed the door in my face and refused to speak to me. I ran after you into the street and begged you for just one word, one sign, anything but the civil death you'd sentenced me to, practically overnight, as if you had glimpsed something inside yourself that you were scared to face.

At that point, I started running in circles around the house like a captive animal.

I'd come and go like a madwoman looking for a sharp object to use on myself.

At that instant, the phone rang.

"Leave right now and don't come back for two hours," Emma ordered, "I'm heading over."

I obeyed. After all, I'd be more likely to run into you outside.

I spent months like this.

I wrote you letters. I'd leave them for you with the doorman of any random building whatsoever, I'd call you at nonexistent phone numbers.

How come you never answered the phone?

I lost weight, I didn't sleep, I'd get out of breath. I'd roam the streets day and night, I'd imagine you turning a corner, reading the paper at a café, getting on the bus. If I could only make you hear me, catch your eye, get a laugh, then you'd let your guard down and I might be able to reach you, it would be just like we were naked again, making love on the floor. Or else, you'd walk into my kitchen again. I was alone, and you opened the refrigerator, which had only one apple in it. In silence, you chewed and decided that you would be in love with me after all. That's how our love began. One girl, one apple, one heart that ventures a bite. The rest, I made up. I awoke crying, as if with your hands on my legs.

Something that resembled my name, but wasn't, arrived then in the center of me.

It's not true, I thought, that an epic of revolution is the same as an epic of love, or that a war of love is the same as a love of war.

It seemed like some things were coming to light: the shouting, the insults in the house.

Nevertheless, the sentence I'm searching for, the most obsessive one, doesn't appear.

Emma watches me bewildered.

I've been living in Rome for a century now, so how am I still in the same house with green walls?

I was taken aback by her lack of insight.

(She didn't realize that the house with green walls was

already a replica of something else.)

Back then, in the office where I worked, there was a cop. Tall guy, kind of a hanger-on. Someone who's a terrorist, has always been, always will be.

Don't you get it, Humboldt? The same sentence I hear in Rome, on this very day, repeated in newspapers, on the radio, on TV, like an infernal lullaby. Today is yesterday, Emma would say. Or to put it another way, time doesn't exist. Humanity, blind as a river. A river of red flags or a river of black flags, it's all the same, because passion, which is colorless, always turns to blood. Putrid Tiber, nameless tomb.

Emma and her false syllogisms. "Fear is an animal. Fear binds us to ideas. Nothing is more dangerous than fear."

I'm trembling, because of what happened, because of what could happen still, because of what never stopped happening. Does longing for freedom intersect at some point with longing for destruction? On the road to action, do ideas become a prison? What sort of idea is a concentration camp?

Humanity blind, like a river. Will this river be the compost heap I steal my poems from? Emma, so tired she's glowing. All of this bores her. She closes her eyes and repeats the inspiration of Silesius: "There is no reason for a rose." And right after that: "You need an invisible requiem for an invisible death."

Why don't I dare to protest?

One morning, I fell brutally ill. I was pale, like someone condemned to death. Then a mild-mannered friend paid me a visit. He brought a notebook where he jotted down the very question I'd been struggling to formulate, and he suggested that we ask the *I Ching*. The copper coins fell on the table.

"The hexagrams aren't wrong. There is a beam running through your being. That's why you surround yourself with the words, the blanks, of a requiem mass. Anyway, one day, on the road that begins where it ends, you'll finally reach failure. At the summit," he said, "the mountain ceases to be a mountain."

But I wasn't really listening, Humboldt. I was distracted by that image of you with your fractured gaze, as if you knew that everything would be taken from you.

Emma in Rome. Emma in her *Requiem for Another Country*.

Rome has an angel that thinks thoughts like, for example, eyes are no more than a square horizon. Rome, as reflected on the river, lacking the courage to exist.

Earthly paradise was this: a senseless, lucid need to leave without having anywhere to go.

Emma: "How long before you start telling a story you don't know."

I don't answer. A lot of time would have to pass before I could even *begin* to stop thinking about you.

Meanwhile I talk, to postpone the final stage of my feelings. (But what is the final stage of my feelings?)

Oh, Humboldt, nobody realizes what Rome takes out of me.

At night, I hear the shrieks of the tortured, it's like my head is about to explode. But that's not going to stop me. I take some Aspirin. It's not going to stop me.

I want everything to blow to smithereens. So language can reveal all the dirt, drool, muck.

Would it help if we cursed like sailors? Why doesn't

everyone just go fuck their fucking selves?

It hadn't occurred to me. To produce an image of myself, out of focus, like Unica Zürn. What I mean is: to commit suicide in a textual sense. Now that would be something. Suicide at the edge of the sewer of the least presentable feelings. Anything but indifference. Indifference is the most cowardly degree of hatred.

An image of the foreign city—Rome, the horrible—protects me.

Where can I lay my head now that you're not here? Where will I be able to stop to sniff a wildflower?

You can hear the sounds of screech owls or barn owls, rising from the *cortile* against the dusk.

"Those guys who helped us set fire to the car dealerships—can we find out where in the hell they ended up?

"Keep it down."

El Bose shakes his head, irritated.

"We have to get the hell *out*, man. This is worse than Cancha Rayada and the CONINTES plan put together. They're screwing with us. And listen to me, it's not just the fascists, it's our own leadership. Disagree on the slightest thing, and they call you a chicken shit, or they accuse you of being ultra-left, or of questioning orders, and, if you're not careful, of supporting imperialism, and then they bring down the Revolutionary Code of Justice on you."

Humboldt's left temple begins to pound.

"What do you mean?"

"I swear on my life," he said crossing his fingers over his mouth, "I swear on Evita, Flag-Bearer of the Poor, I witnessed it: first the crimes, then the punishments, then the proceedings."

Humboldt thinks, no way, he's drunk. But El Bose is only half finished.

"Hold on, I'm not done . . . extreme liberalism, desertion in the face of the enemy, several degrees of insubordination, and . . . having sexual relations outside of wedlock!"

Humboldt can't hold back a smile.

"Seems like you're going to have to rethink your practices with the girls, man."

"Fuck you, man, you just don't get it. You never got it. For your information, everything I did, I did because I wanted to. Not because of Trotskyism or voluntarism or masochism, like other guys. At first I was having a little too much fun, sure, I'll be the first to admit it. I spent money on clothes, girls threw themselves at me. But soon enough, I was up to my balls, and nobody worried about my class background when it came time to nail an operation. Besides, I was my own worst critic. I'll never try to justify—never, you hear me?—our use of imprisonment, exile, and the firing squad against our own ranks, for any reason."

"So what are you going to do?"

"Nothing. I haven't got a pot to piss in, I don't have a scrap of legit indentification, I don't have a house, I don't even have a place to lay my own dead body, and on top of that, when I tried to raise the issue, they told me I was on my own. What am I supposed to do?"

Humboldt didn't know what to say and grew distracted.

I've always been interested in people, he thinks. But not all people, of course, not people who think that the country ends at the corner of Córdoba and Callao. Sometimes, at night, when I can't sleep, my life seems like one big screw-up. Like I committed a crime against myself. Or something like that. She's all I have, she's more real than me. I'm, at best, an accident. But still, I have to admit that I don't understand her. I watch her come and go, considering several paths, as if they were all the same, and I never know which one she's going to take, or if she'll take one at all, or if maybe she's really going, in all her motionless wandering, nowhere. And all of that, with an innocent, cruel look on her face, with that severity that I'd wanted to soften in her and can't, because it's the very form her life takes, her way of grabbing hold of her own mystery. She loves what she doesn't understand. Sometimes she pretends to be other people. Sometimes she throws herself into new experiences like someone in a tragic last ditch effort to live, and then she fixates on the climax, on those states at the brink of death where a person, paradoxically, is most alive.

When I met her, I thought that, underneath, there was a girl as fragile as a crystal vase. Now I think she was born to hurt herself, cruelly, to soak up every last drop of her rich inner emptiness like poisonous nectar. Politics is only one of the names for this desire. Otherwise her life is full of inconsequential stuff—me, for instance.

"Hey man, are you listening to me or what?"

The Will asked: "Remember when we all went to Ezeiza singing: *Cry, cry / fucking oligarchy?* We were visionaries, man, visionaries!"

"This chick acts like she's in the Worker's Party," The Word House mumbled to the side. She couldn't stand The Will, she could hardly stomach the sight of her.

"Why don't you go screw yourself?" retorted The Will, who heard. "What were you doing when Evita announced her historical renunciation?"

"Drinking milk from a bottle."

"And where were you when Perón came back and the first shots started flying?"

"I fled to Mexico."

"Shut up then."

(The Will was burning up, but she didn't take off her little Ban-Lon cardigan.)

Longing thought, how come I stopped dancing to *Pata Pata* by Miriam Makeba? Oh, I used to love *Modart en la Noche*!

"Perón or Homeland, Long Live Death," shouted Nobody, returning from the bathroom. "I just passed one of the People's Revolutionary Army freaks in the doorway. He says he belongs to an organization which has been declared illegal."

"Did he say anything else?"

"Yeah, that something like a Pinochet-style coup is on the way."

The Wasp looked up from the Civil Code and flashed his freckled face. He was chubby, The Wasp. And sometimes he wiped one hand over his face, like so.

"Why don't we decide once and for all who will participate in the Dorrego Operation?"

"I'd rather go to Itacombú," Longing said.

"Ha, I knew it!" said The Word House. "You can't fool me, sweetie. A little birdie told me that you had a crush on an architecture student in that camp. . ."

Longing frowned.

"Yeah, I forget his name. You don't think they could have killed him, do you? After we made love, he gave me a kiss on the forehead and walked out, just like that. I never saw him again."

Huddled in her corner, The Soul thought about how Longing suffered, and how that suffering came from far away, even farther away than childhood.

Let someone guide her, she prayed.

Let someone carry her to bed tonight.

And once they get to the bed, help her take off her shoes and get undressed and then ask her: My darling, what *is* it between you and your name? Are you a synonym of your name? Or maybe a failed metaphor, or a semantic shift? What will your name be next Monday, or next year, or in the next world?

Above all, don't forget to pull the covers up, it's cold, and her heart is grieving.

Let somebody leave her like that, on the shores of wherever she has always been heading, increasingly blind, increasingly naked, increasingly open.

Praise to you, Madonna del Parto.

"I don't get it."

"What don't you get? I'm happy to explain everything again, if you like: the difference between government and power, the university of the people, class struggle and the form that it assumes at every stage . . . but first, you have to tell me who the hell you are, man, because while we sit here and shoot the intellectual shit, the agro-export bourgeoisie, multinational corporations, and imperialists aren't exactly scratching their balls."

"I don't get what in hell's name is happening *now*."

"Same as always, when the masses are on the rise, repression kicks in even harder, that's all."

"And what's the Doctrine of Military Occupation?"

"Same thing as the Doctrine of the Counterinsurgency or the Doctrine of National Security: a politics directed at younger officers, and run by none other than the Pentagon. But don't forget that there are still internal contradictions in the army. The army is liable to split between the progressives and the imperialists. That's the thing we have to watch for, because that moment will be crucial."

"You mean, the army could side with the Progressives?"

"Possibly."

"But most of the officers—who are they with?"

"The Pentagon."

"Oh."

They said that they couldn't use firing squads, The Wasp explained. That they couldn't enact a program of daily mass killings. They couldn't leave behind any evidence, blood, bodies, because then the pesky questions would start, like, for example, who is the perpetrator? How was it done? When?

This way, what evidence could be brought to light? Better this, while society stands divided, detached from itself, hushed up. Nothing seen, nothing heard. The sum total of public power swallowed it, a gaping dead zone in history. Strikes, fight plans, riots, factory occupations, fires, expropriated funds, bombs? Forget all that, they said. We will impose *in*-security. We're going to operate off the political radar. We'll put ourselves under the command of The Most Eminent Armed Forces for Repression, the Criminal Junta, Filthy Prince Jorge Rafael Videla of the Little Mustaches and Moral Mendacity. Just like that, more unified than ever, stronger, better established than ever, we'll erase their names, we'll deny their whereabouts, we'll eradicate every trace of them, we won't acknowledge what happened, and we'll proclaim, with our heads held high: We've completed our mission, Long Live Elusive History.

They said, according to The Wasp, that no one will be able to deny, under any circumstances, our linguistic contribution, our worthy donation to the national language, in the form of a national swamp.

The list was unreal, The Wasp said. They'd left scores of toxic, literally unpalatable words. A real shit heap, he said. Then he started enumerating what his memory, in an unprecedented effort, had retained, and all of that, amid the stench of the military and a broken conscience.

As *civitas* of the national nightmare, they said, it's not bad. (They seemed, The Wasp said, genuinely proud.)

Memory will be scratching in the dark, they said. Where can you look for *what is neither dead nor still alive?* Where, if they aren't where you thought? On what hallowed ground of the exiled community? In what anagram of the unheard?

Patriotic Mission Accomplished, they said. Long Live Liberated Repression.

Let them do, they said, or think whatever they like. Let them have their Museum of the Dead, their marches, their wasteland of love, their psychological dilemmas, and their whole quagmire. Let them organize vigils or stop, in the middle of the world, to rebuke us. We couldn't care less. We won. The flag will spit flames over their ruins.

"Back to the night of the failed Annunciation . . ." said Athanasius.

I quickly cut him off.

"First I want to hear about you. Who you are, why you're here, why you're interested in all this."

The little old man looked at me kindly. Apparently my curiosity flattered him.

"Well, Miss, I was born in Germany, not far from Mainz, in 1602. I had to grow up during the Thirty Years War, or in other words, in a world full of fear, fanaticism, and ideological debate, not terribly different from this one. I studied Hebrew, physics, and mathematics, as well as *Syntagma Musicum* by Praetorius, who was a disciple of Giordano Bruno. Still rather young, I had my disagreements with Trithemius of Würzburg, a sort of Prospero who knew about necromancy and communicated without difficulty with the seven intelligences of God. Shortly after, I observed sun spots with a telescope, and I published my first book, *Ars Magnesia*, while teaching in Avignon. In the Year of Our Lord's Favor 1635, I arrived in Rome, where I was received by the Barberini family, and I had the feeling of making my entrance in the Great Theater of the World by the hand of Giulio Camillo, or rather, in a Theatrum Polydicticum that, as you know, is a chamber where one can see paradises, fabulous treasures, and endless libraries. From that moment on, I have never left that place (so to speak), except to gather materials for my Museum. I have an unusual memory. My teachers have been, always, Archimedes, Philo of Byzantium, Proclus, Iamblichus, Agrippa von Nettesheim, and Hero of Alexandria. I am also interested in the texts of the Second Scholasticism, the arts of *curiosae*, problems of acoustics, and above all, images that, expertly fabricated, can turn into amulets and guide us to the light. I count among my proudest accomplishments my friendship with Gian Lorenzo Bernini and having attended the first performance of Monteverdi's *L'Orfeo*. To conclude . . . I consider myself fortunate: I have seen two or three things for the first time, and I believe I have always sought the answer to a single question: how to live. Is that enough?"

"I think so," I had no choice but to assent.

The monk sighed with satisfaction.

"In that case . . . if you permit me, Miss, I would like to return to Emma. That night, in fact, your friend could not sleep. She awoke and put the kettle on the stove to make some tea, and the water boiled, thank God. And then she heard some noises coming from the landing, but she was not afraid."

. . .

"Do you happen to know anything about the scene of the Annunciation?" he asked abruptly.

His question seemed out of place, and I was about to respond that I didn't know much about it, but he didn't give me time.

"Every Annunciation contains three mysteries," he said, "the Angel's appearance, his greeting, and the colloquy. A different shade of blue corresponds to each mystery: lapis lazuli powder, cupric carbonate, and ultramarine, respectively. The scene occurs on Friday, at sunrise, on an altarpiece. Or better yet, in a room with a baldachin. Or on a threshold, with a pantheon behind it, a city behind it, an infinite garden behind it, one occupied by Adam and Eve, also infinitely, exiled. Or in a shadowy interior, like in a church, in which a tiny Christ arrives from Heaven with a cross in his hand, or rather, dangling from the beak of the Holy Spirit in a cradle that is also a boat, or rather like a golden rain softly entering Mary's womb through a porthole, and all of this occurs in Nazareth, which means flower. *Blessed art thou*, and then it depends: the Virgin swings among the *perturbatio, interrogatorio*, and *obedientia*. And that, no matter whether her figure appears on the right, on the left, inside or outside the room, standing or seated on a throne, in ecstasy or scurrying away like a cat, with her breasts bare or her legs spread open, holding a missal or the Book of Isaiah, which contains the prophecy of the very thing happening at that moment, or completely uninterested in the book or the angel, with interlaced fingers and a halo, repeating the words of Luke: *Look at me, I am the Lord's servant.*"

The little old man paused to take a breath.

"Oh," he sighed, "if Emma had been born in Rome in 1646, she would have been no stranger to the secrets of variety and the ornate, the *Libro degli strumenti di martirio*, the argument of images, the sensible quality of Paradise, the treaty entitled *Statua*, which resolves problems of proportion according to the law of thirds, the thirteen marvels that link the body with everything, and the idea of total vision, capable of containing, in an inseparable unity, infinite perspectives, as was formulated by Nicolás de Cusa in *On the Vision of God*, or *On Painting*. I mean, she would have been able to choose, far more simply, to paint the Angel: effeminate, barefoot, with tricolor wings, shooting two beams from his eyes at Mary, with a lyre in his hand, with Latin words leaving his mouth in phylacteries written in reverse so that God can read them."

Suddenly a suspicion shook me: the monk was just killing time before announcing—he, this time—something terrible.

The question came out bitter.

"What was the date?"

Athanasius scratched his head. "March 11, 1976."

I knew it, I thought.

"It's important to understand, Miss, that on that morning, Emma knew something that you still don't. She knew it in a slippery, fleeting way, perhaps, but she knew it. And all of it lent grace to that Annunciation that, according to her limited perspective, she had ruined. Let's assume she thought that, in those words written on the canvas—in the stain that they amounted to—there was Death, and that Death, in its way, also carried a message. It came, carrying in its hand, instead of a lilly, the never-ending burden of violence, poverty, and confusion that corresponds to every exiled creature in the world. And that's not bad, thought Emma, not *necessarily* bad, because what are terror and punishment but the reverse of compassion and surrender, and they are indispensable to the appreciation of the beauty (wisdom) of the ephemeral. She didn't know how or where she had reached this certainty, which exalted her with some combination of joy and terrifying pain. And, nevertheless, she couldn't sustain that grace. She couldn't tolerate its clarity. Maybe for that reason, she turned to prayer (which is one of the paradoxical forms of distraction), and I heard her say:

"Protect me, my God, from the figure of the Hero, ffrom all prisons, including the people's prisons, from all this nonsense about the means and the end, from the verb 'to re-educate', from purity that is noxious, from the tragic ease with which good people can turn, just like that, into executioners, from men with no imagination whose mouths are full of contempt and whose eyes never laugh, and in general, from those who think, without even flinching, that the best enemy is the dead enemy. Never let me forget, not under any circumstances, that violence is fascist, always. And help me to be more like Lippi, who painted with my favorite shade of blue and was also an orphan, like every artist."

I was late to realize, Humboldt, the *unnatural* chastity with which I politicized. When I say "politicized," I'm referring to politics, poetry, my suffragette shoes. I'm also referring to you, Humboldt, to you most of all. It's as if, absorbed in frozen purity, aiming nowhere, I would have always lived deaf, and tacitly indifferent, to every request.

My Private Life tells me to buy some new clothes, go out, get a haircut. Whatever it takes to avoid that empty feeling, she says. But emptiness is something full—how can you add any more nothing to nothing? I mean, at night, naked in bed, I stroke my breasts, one hand, then two, as if I were, indeed, Baudelaire's whore. I tell myself, if I've at least achieved extreme repulsion between the poem and my body, then maybe *something* could materialize. So I close my eyes, wet my lips with my tongue. Something creeps through the darkness like a beast that has awoken suddenly in a dream. The dream rears up, and it is you. In solitude, pleasure takes on a confusing flavor, I leave myself, to reach myself, with no alibi but you (or my memory of you), and a repertoire of scenes that I fabricated. True, illicit enrichment, that archive, made of false pieces that never stop combining, without your consent. For example, you and I coming home from a party, still drinking, passing ice cubes from mouth to mouth (I always loved how you kissed, Humboldt), and right then and there, on the kitchen floor, every dip, curve, inch of my body, you wait for me, I urge you on, you feel me, and then you take me all the way from start to finish, from the nape of my neck to my feet, from never to always. Or maybe you're reading the newspaper in your olive green sweater and I, determined to distract you, kiss you (behind your ears), guide your hand under my dress, and you don't even flinch, which drives me wild (I never knew if you did that on purpose—acted indifferent, I mean), until everything blurs, Humboldt, because it's suddenly as if you were writing on my body, up, down, and in circles, and I don't know how to ask you to stop, though desire is unbearable.

Oh Humboldt. I leave these scenes destroyed (but in no way purified) by sobs. Like a little girl who, left to her tantrum, gives up on whatever she wanted out of sheer exhaustion.

And then, nothing. It is always still the same night, the night you're not there, when I speak these useless words to no one but myself.

"That's no good," My Private Life said.

Am I really not doing it right? Yes. No. I don't know. I should reread Baudelaire. That might help. It might explain why I can't write and can't *not* write and, at the end of the day, why I go on without even knowing who I am. Wasn't I many different people for you, Humboldt? One name after the other, and yet no one. Love is a hard drug, a friend of mine once said. So is poetry, I thought. Writing is deadly for a woman. A good number kill themselves, all of them cry, all of them live the romantic night of abandon and take pills and then sleep forever, like Sleeping Beauty of the Forest.

Except there are no poems in the forest. In the forest, there are only trees, and hummingbirds, and deer that scamper up to eat apples. In the forest, only an absolute reality exists, the abyssal richness of what is, without us, before and after time.

I forget what I was going to say.

Oh, yeah, the same old thing: you come over, and it's Sunday, and it's raining, and we make love, surrounded by police. And while we make love, the police stand at attention, their leather boots right up against my ears, at the same time my friends repeat over and over that I should just forget you, as if that concept—to forget you—fit inside the night, inside *our* night, Humboldt, packed with armored cars, where we lose everything, above all, what we hoped to be. And nobody knows, Humboldt, nobody other than you and I know the sheer effort of things, of every little piece of life torn from death, every battle that we fought, including the real forest of the impossible, where desire *always* craves something it shouldn't.

No. I'm not going to wake up, Humboldt. I swear to you on the city of Rome. Who knows. Maybe this way, I'll have an idealized image of us. (Which would be like telling a story without telling it.) They say you only need a short inciting fragment. Some fleeting image, mildly erotic, that resembles a dream or a war. War is a kind of divination, they say. Someone tosses the dice at random. In the *cortile*, you can hear a very sweet song. (Everything immediately preceding death is sweet.) The song is titled: "Me and My Desire Under the Red Stars." It's a naive title, quite clearly deceitful.

Always, and in every place, Death sees its own kind.

"So what were you doing all that time, if I may ask?"

Athanasius received my question with infinite patience.

"I was nervous, too. I remember how, to distract myself, I began thinking of Rome. I knew that I would return sometime very soon, and it occurred to me that I might establish a special club for members of the Museum. I would call it The Ulysses Laboratory. To gain membership, interested parties would have to answer the following questions: What is the difference between the Tower of Babel and the oldest minaret in Islam? How do you purge the brain of a wise man? Which of the world's doors open to the Waters of Fortune? How many triangles fit into the sphere of love?"

The little old man scratched his head.

He then showed me a mysterious book that I had never before seen in his possession.

It was a copy of the *Treatise on the Dialogical Universal*, which according to him addresses, in the guise of the angel Cosmiel and the ecstatic rapture of Theodactus, the stupendous machine of the world and the question, "Why, in life, are all beautiful things distant?"

"But what about Emma?" I insisted. "What happened then?"

"Ah," the old man sighed as if suddenly overcome with exhaustion. "In the parlor, Death appeared, disguised as Death. But I didn't notice. The only thing I saw was a raven, which reminded me of Edgar Allan Poe, who in turn reminded me of the beating of a buried heart, which reminded me of Orpheus, wearing jeans, singing rock n' roll."

"It's been a while since you've given me the time of day," said The Word House, in an injured tone.

Longing tried to explain herself.

"It's just that The Will was treating me like a lackey, sending me on errands all over the place, she told me to study the constitution, wear the cockade of Argentina, to stop loafing around. Besides, I'm nervous because I have no idea what I'm writing. That's worrying me. Lately everything is so democratic that the result is frightful. They confuse me, they devalue my thoughts, they steal my ideas!"

"Who does?"

"It doesn't matter who, they copied my work!"

The Word House decided to change the subject.

"You want to grab something to eat? Nothing like leaving the theater of operations for a little while."

"What? Has the war against the subversives flared up again?"

"No, silly, that war is over."

"Oh, good," Longing said with an utter lack of conviction. "I wanted to ask you a question. You know how we lied about everything, our names, jobs, PO boxes? Do you think we were like professional con men?

"Your problem is that you never remember anything. That's why you go through life trying to go back and, meanwhile, you never end up where you think."

"You have a point. I don't even know how I got into Marxism."

Not by reading *Alice in Wonderland*, thought The Word House.

At that, the rest of them appeared at the door of the café. The Word House felt like she'd been rescued.

"Did I tell you guys about my dream that Officer Margaride searched the Student Union?"

"That's awful," said The Wasp.

"No, but nothing awful happened. They lined us up against the wall, frisked us, and charged us with illicit organizing, public intimidation, possession of explosives, and multiple counts of disturbing the peace. Then they hauled us to jail—a *legal* jail, can you believe that? We were *très chanceaux*."

"And how many years did we rot away in prison?"

"Eight."

"Listen," said The Wasp, without lifting his eyes from the newspaper. "The government vowed not to do business with common delinquents. Isabelita just decreed the state of siege to protect school-aged children."

A commanding voice echoed through the café.

"I annihilate, you annihilate, he annihilates, we

annihilate."

"And what's that?" asked The Unknown.

"The National Broadcast."

"It's perfectly clear," said one high-ranking hotshot who came by to deliver the orders, "that this is all part of the grand plan, put in place by the army and the reactionaries, to intimidate and demobilize workers. But they had better realize, if the country isn't governed by the people, then the people won't be governed by anyone. There's no way around it. It's Attack and Assault. We believe that a National Liberation Front, sooner or later, can rise to power."

"Come on, guys," The Soul interrupted. "Today is March, 11, 1976. I just turned eighteen. I'm not interested in beauty, only in its unreality. Look at me – I'm ready to be!"

Poor thing, thought The Word House, always in the stratosphere, always sliding *de soi-même en soi-même*.

The Will, meanwhile, felt like a fifth wheel. She thought: What can I do today, Tuesday, at 6:45 in the evening, to advance class struggle?

Things accelerated for no apparent reason. People everywhere went on strike, at General Motors, Bendix, Ford, Propulsora Siderúrgica, the Minimax supermarkets, Fate, Sitrac-Sitram, Astarsa, the Lisandro de la Torre meatpacking plant.

"This just goes to show how when the people are mobilized, they're unstoppable," shouted someone from the Movement For Socialism.

On TV there was word of a subversive killed in a shooting. He was thought to be responsible for a recent attempt on the life of an admiral. The capture of his accomplices was supposedly imminent.

"You haven't said anything in ages. What's wrong, sweetie? What do you make of all this?"

"To form an opinion, I'd have to know what's really going on in the country."

"What country?"

"This one—where else?"

"Okay, here's a summary: Things have gone to shit. And don't even dream of going out for a haircut, every idiotic little thing costs you an arm and a leg, and this is a mess no one can fix …"

"The workers didn't become Peronists for this," The Wasp concluded.

Evita, already dead, was shouting.

"My little darlings, my sweet little flea-bitten rag-pickers: I was once a little sparrow in a swarm of sparrows. And he, a condor soaring high and proud over the hills. I was the student, he was the teacher. I was the shadow, he was the figure. I'll sing his name, so that I might never feel like an oligarch. Never leave us, dear Perón. Draw round Perón, my darling little vermin. Whether or not we spill their blood, the oligarchy will die out in this century."

"Great Queen of Peronism. There's nobody quite like her, when it comes to shielding our Leader from sellouts and imperialists, on the Right or Left!" said one loyal subject.

"Personally, I love how she speaks so familiarly to men, just like Victoria Ocampo," said The Word House.

As for Longing, her thoughts were elsewhere.

"Did you see how, at the march in Tucumán, everyone was shouting *Long live the army?*"

"What do you expect, kiddo? Une véritable horreur."

Nobody thought about the disaster in Taco Ralo and turned his head.

The rest of them wore a neutral expression, and even The Soul appeared lost in thought.

Over Buenos Aires, in the middle of March, a deadly snow began to fall.

All of it lovely and somewhat absurd.

This man, I thought, will drive me crazy.

The clock read eight. On what day, what year, in what city?

Athanasius divined my thought.

"At 8 o'clock," he said, "a comma is a comma, but in quantum theory, you never know. Eight is a peculiar hour, poorly brought up and a bit quarrelsome: she's easily offended, she changes moods as quickly as she changes dresses, especially in summer."

He inserted an almost theatrical pause.

"In Rome for example, at eight o'clock, solitude is at work, as is nostalgia for oneself."

I closed my eyes without realizing.

If I try hard enough, I told myself, maybe I'll make it to the empty center of these tautologies where something can happen. (Sometimes, Humboldt, the unexpected does occur.) You, for example, arrive and explain what happened, tidy up, put everything in the right box, remember to breathe, you tell me, tomorrow I'll look for that little earring you lost. (You should have said, I'm going to find the self you lost in a world with no objects.)

When I opened my eyes, I thought I might be dreaming: I saw a shadow pass by carrying a copy of Heidegger's *Being and Time*.

The little old man was still talking, but now with more reserve, as if he sensed he was about to offend me.

"As you know, Miss, on this eleventh of March at eight o'clock, Death was at Humboldt's heels. She had begun to be follow him just as he and El Bose parted ways. She was somewhat disenchanted, because *this* Humboldt, she thought, was *not* Humboldt. That man, she had met in 1769. And what an extraordinary character! He studied herbaria, coral reefs, plant taxonomy, the comparative study of catastrophes and, above all, young men. In sum, the *kosmos* and *naturphilosophen*. This guy, on the other hand, had never climbed the Chimborazo, nor did he possess a library of 17,000 volumes, nor was he capable of drawing a picturesque travel atlas. He was no lover of linguistics, isothermal lines, or the kindred emotions of axolotls. No relation to Charles-Marie de la Condamine.

And, yet, Death still found him intriguing.

What she liked most about him were his hands.

And his mystic ability to persevere in error."

For the Union Lawyer, today is also March 11, 1976. A day is a day, from start to finish, even March 11, 1976. He spent a sleepless night fulfilling his duty. And yet, he thinks, the night's not over yet. Despite the light (it's eight o'clock), night lives on inside of me and won't really be over until I get this letter down on paper, until I manage to say what my heart and every bone in my body resist saying, even though it's necessary, oh, my orange desert, I'll be kept away from you, not allowed to touch or breathe you for a very long time, so long it might be forever, my hands won't touch your body, your Annunciation won't find me, I need you to understand this, I don't have any choice, it would be unforgivable, totally unforgivable if the sands of the Sahara, my little nirvana, were lost on my account, because of some lonely act while searching for the blue of the word *homeland*, just like the blue in your Annunciations, because blue is nothing more than a human sliver of the absolute that everyone, at some point, inexplicably desires. What I mean is, Death is breathing down my neck, I am, we are, in a moment of defeat, I won't ask you to forgive me, I'll try to forgive myself, no revolution would ever be won if anything happened to you . . . oh my love, how can a caravan escape the desert.

All of those thoughts, and it is still March 11, 1976, it is still (just after) eight o'clock.

"My dear:

No one escapes their own death.

It's possible, though, to choose how you die. To pass through death, as it passes through you, with total clarity.

My whole life has been no more than the development of this idea.

Let's just say that, like Graham Greene's priest, I ceded something that never was, to something that could never be. And at that instant, paradise was no longer stuck in the past, and I could share the miracle of brotherhood with other men, as if it were a loaf of bread. It wasn't hard. There was a generosity in the air. A politically radical climate. The world cut perfectly clean into two halves. Here they are, these are them: our weapons of the absolute. Only a man resigned to his death can experience the mystery of his humanity. What's utopia anyway, if not an intensification of oneself? We're so small without that strength, without that clarity that leads us into love and battle, if they're not one and the same.

Then, as if something were missing from my life, an orange desert stretched out before me.

How dazzling you were!

My lady, I said, do you want to share this feeling with me? If you'll allow me, I said, I'll tell you who I am and, more important, who I've been and hope to be. I'll show you where I'm going, who I'm going with, and why. I'll tell you about the world I'm bound for. Remember when I talked at night, by the light of a smoldering cigarette? Going over the history of the country, for hours, explaining events, picking them apart, reconstructing them: the secret deal with Frondizi, combative labor unions, the politics of the Great National Agreement, armed groups, Taco Ralo and Garín, until there was nothing left to say, no stone in the resistance movement left unturned. What about Perón? you asked. And I came back with a quote from John William Cooke: Peronism is the repugnant curse of the bourgeois country. Without a working class, there could be no revolution, and here the working class is Peronist. Who gives a damn about Perón? The important thing is to create the conditions for revolution. Then the Old Man will have to accept it, whether he likes it or not, if he doesn't want to cease to be Perón, just watch how he'll hop onto our backs. And other times I'd recite you passages from Macbeth, King Lear, all of

Shakespeare's bleakness and dismal pride, plus some of his furious happiness. That's how I used to talk about the future, which looks just like the past, but no matter, because along the way, life that gives life stands in opposition to life that gives death, and one may dream about the freedom of all men, and it was like losing myself again in the folds of your body.

   You have to believe me. What I'm feeling now isn't fear. At most it's an excruciating, stabbing awareness that I'm going to desert you in the middle of an infected wound, full of hushed things that will never ascend into speech.

   It's agony to imagine you in empty parks, in a thirsty country, where the faces from our biography have never been, when you're suddenly gripped by terror, scorched, hooded, erased, negated, relocated, burned, skewered, sucked up, split open, riddled, blown off, tossed out, and left manacled, mutilated, destroyed, recoiling, blindfolded, in a ditch, a field, on a piece of bare ground, in a dump, a sewer, an abandoned car, with the Ithacas still ringing out, the voices that scream *Run, bitch*, it's too painful even to imagine, but our love, my little nirvana, will never be held hostage, or taken as the spoils of war, I guarantee that, they'll never get their hands on it, no matter how they search for us, not even when they find us, our bodies in the night of all time, because the desert is undiscoverable, my lady, and what we were looking for was the thirst itself, not just the knowledge of thirst, which would already be to quench it.

   But I know I still have something to explain. What you found sewn into the lining of my pants was the result of a mature, rational decision. If you accept the premise that nothing exalts a man more than rebellion, then nothing reduces and bestializes him more than submission to those in power. That's why I carry the pill. I carry it to protect myself from, at the very least, moral degradation, so the victory of never being taken alive, of being able to say in the end *You didn't kill me, death was my choice* is in my own hands. It'll be soon, I know. And I know that I'm alive right now, for all the life I won't have later. And that my death will be great, like a sun storm, and it will be meaningful, because the historical project that I've died for will go on. How could popular struggle die out? Who could halt its unstoppable march?

I've never been happier, I want you to know that. I also want you to know that I wear a sign right on my forehead that reads *Thinking is done here*. Or better yet, *Oppositional Thinking Is Done Here*. That includes, of course, thinking against myself. "Myself" is the dreamer; he's also the one who is suspicious of power, regardless of sides. I can't imagine a more fundamental right than the right to dissent.

In other words, my lady, nothing infuriates me more than injustice, though I consider submission and subservience, which are forms of foolishness, equally intolerable. That's why I live like this, at the mercy of passion, and by passion I mean one of the links connecting us to truth (the other one is disintegration).

We happened on bad times, but no worse than others. Anguish, exploitation, the thousand faces of human misery, and the word *homicides* (which has plenty of synonyms, all inadequate to define the waste of life that they stand for) are more than 'social' evils. As for our alleged defeat, we'll always have that quote from Rémusat, and don't ever forget it: *Les échecs de la vérité ne m'ont point réconcilié avec le faux.*

As for our love, you know as well as I do that it's

weighted down with obstacles. But I want to tell you something. No matter what, I would never trade it for anything. I'm saying that I'm going to fight for it until the end. Our first times together were enough ecstasy and wonder to last me forever. Nothing can make that not exist.

My love: if John William Cooke rose from the dead, he wouldn't want to die. He'd immediately stand up and keep fighting. That's my plan. I have long days ahead, I know. I'll suffer knowing how far away you are, but there is no way I'll go back on my feelings. My love for you is like a vehement oath: it can't be suspended and doesn't accept limitations, the sponge never dries. Take my insistence, the protest of my loyalty, my impending nostalgia. I love you intensely, lucidly."

"What now? Who's going to say what happened next?"

"Not me," Longing said, "I have no part in any of this. Leave me be. Not to mention I'm kind of scared."

"What of?" The Unknown asked.

"Of betraying a dream, of censoring myself, of risking too much, of being spotted by one of the men who still roam freely in Buenos Aires. You can fill in the blanks."

"You're right. Time passed, and everything is exactly like it was before. Exactly."

"What if we go back to the *Moyen Âge* in Rome?" interjected The Word House, who loved masks.

"No," said The Unknown, "She'd flop as an artist."

"Who?" asked Longing.

"You. Didn't anyone ever tell you that artists are supposed to throw themselves into their art, whatever it takes, at any cost?

"I don't get it," said Longing, "is the problem political or aesthetic?"

"Both," said The Unknown, "art is also, above all, the confused, magnificent, impossible relationship between Truth and Beauty."

"Oh," Longing cried, not even pretending to understand.

"You just have to close your eyes and jump. Who cares if you air your dirty laundry, or become a moving target for repression, or if the right exploits you, or the left derides you … it's the only way," he concluded.

"Look," he added after a pause, "I'm going to help you out a little: Tuesday, March 11, 1976, after he left the café, after writing his letter to Emma, the Union Lawyer, Roberto Sinigaglia, C.I. 5.945.321, was abducted outside his studio at 1362 Lavalle. It was 10:25. Several pedestrians, cab drivers, and bus drivers witnessed the event in passing. They observed how some fifteen men in plain clothes got out of their green Ford Falcons, and closed in on him like a clamp, and by shoving and threatening him, flashing long and short weapons, they forced him face down on the floor in the backseat of one car, but not before he screamed his name, as if his name were in itself an accusation and could protect him from *whatever* was, inevitably, happening in broad daylight, before the shocked eyes of people who couldn't, or maybe didn't wish to, comprehend it, and the cars suddenly flying down Lavalle. And that was it. No media outlet, print or radio, not that day, or the next, or the following week, or the following year or any year after, reported the fact. Nobody knew where they took him or what became of him. Nobody submitted an inquiry. No power, judicial or otherwise, assured his physical integrity. Nobody stood vigil over his body. Nobody buried him. It was a bright morning, and somewhat sad, like all March mornings in Buenos Aires."

Longing lowered her head.

The Word House also gave thanks, without even knowing what she was grateful for, without understanding why a voice inside of her, a bit hoarse, was saying, *Come on, damn it!*

And Death laughs.

And Athanasius, who adores the gratuitousness of games but not gratuitous games, would like to ask her: Didn't you have a childhood? Don't you find all this grieving a bit upsetting? What kind of revolution are you interested in? Are you the perfect opposite of desire, or the tranquility of what we have yet to accept?

And Death laughs.

And Athanasius opens the newspaper and reads:

"At five o'clock today, security forces carrying out a patrol in Quilmes were besieged by a rebel group. Resisting the attack, they managed to shoot down two subjects whose identities have not been determined."

And Death laughs.

And Athanasius continues: "Army forces blast down extremist in Córdoba. Five members of the Heroic Vietnam group die in Tucumán. In La Plata, a suspect is killed when a bomb he was carrying detonates. Six terrorists fall while attempting escape. Six more in Rosario. One more in B.A."

And Death laughs.

And in the darkness of the parlor, it dawns on March 11, 1976.

And Emma tosses in bed, without knowing that, in next apartment, a young man is dreaming about becoming a public accountant.

And Athanasius prays in supplication: "Oh Abraxas, relieve us, like the nilometer, of all adversity and catastrophe . . . And if for some reason you cannot, then help us to accept that the gods move men like puppets, and the most that we can hope for, as Irenaeus teaches so well in his book on Gnostic errors, is to hold the most beautiful poses."

And nothing else happens, except maybe a minor tremor in the memory of some god, producing that perfect mixture of intelligence and necessity that is required, according to Plotinus, for the Absolute Circular Journey to become the Art of Reality.

And Death laughs. And steps forward wearing a pink hat or something.

And she says, perhaps, *Fossils*. Or: *I am walking towardsshadows*. Or: *The outer walls of a child in the multitudes of a man*.

And a few toy soldiers appear, all in a row, like illusions battling in a climate of hate, among relics and a smattering of necessary language, one with no grammar yet.

"Had she been able," the little old man assured, "before the summary had been requested, and long before the judge ordered the documents to deliver his sentence, Emma would have no doubt appeared to testify and, in the transcription corresponding to such and such folios, of such and such case book being presented before number such and such Federal Penal Court, of such and such division, the official in charge would have transcribed her words more or less as follows:

A revolutionary Peronist, like John William Cooke. Yeah, that's him. He always wore a tie. Collar upturned. He bites his nails. People call him The Monk, because he looks like the priest in *The Power and the Glory* by Graham Greene. He has a watch that was a gift from Fidel, he told me that one day when we went for tea with his aunt Lola. As far as I know, he doesn't have a house, or he had several. Sometimes he would stay with me one night and then disappear for weeks. My heart is in my throat just thinking about it. That night he told me that he was going to sleep in Boulogne or in Villa Ballester, I don't remember which. Things aren't going too well, he said. Militant training in Cuba? Yeah, he worries about the question of God. No, he didn't come from Tacuara. His best friend, Carlitos, who had a thin mustache just like Dalí, had fought in Algeria. Date of birth? November 6, but I don't know the year. He went to a boarding school run by priests. No, he's not an orphan. I don't know why. Juan Pablo Maestre and Mirta Misetich? Yeah, sure, he recited Shakespeare by heart, he loves to read. No, it was back in the days of the Federal Penal Chamber, when the death squads were avenging the killing of a some captain. That day, somebody had spotted him sitting in La Giralda, he was there until 10. I'm sure they beat him silly. Sons of bitches. They shoved him. His eyes would be glassy with the pain.

Yes, I feel alright. A night owl. Ascetic. Extraordinary man. They were waiting for him. They made sure that no legal police were in the area, so they could calmly go about their business. No thanks, I have a lawyer, I'm going to present a habeas corpus. To which authorities? Yes, I'd appreciate that. Campo de Mayo, Comisaría 19, Cementerio Fluvial, La Pecera, Pozo de Banfield, Sheraton Matanza. I understand. The important thing is to prevent, legalize, struggle for, determine, demand his immediate. What was that? Right here? Of course."

Athanasius stopped suddenly and scratched his head. "It was still March 11, 1976," he said.

"It was still only just after 8, and the Union Lawyer was composing a letter. Emma sprung up in bed. What time is it? Why isn't the phone ringing? Didn't he say he was going to call?

She decided to get up.

On the table several sketches of the Annunciation attested to her patience and perhaps also to her curious gift for adversity.

The boy who dreamed about becoming a public accountant yawned again.

Farther away, on la avenida Santa Fe, someone with a poor vocabulary and a vast abyss of nameless things headed straight for the apartment on Uruguay.

His years of service were limited, but not his intuition or expertise in detecting Marxists in schools, pizzerias, neighborhood council meetings, intensive care units, student unions, groups of psychoanalysts.

He advanced armed, in dark glasses, confident in his ability to execute kidnappings and killings.

Armed, he advanced.

Softly crooning the theme song to *If you know it, sing*, or some other infamous invention of the Doctrine of National Security."

"What confusion, *mon Dieu!*" said The Word House, "Do you have any idea what's happening?"

"Sure," The Soul injected in a small voice. "Without realizing it, we've arrived at a dangerous corner of History. . ."

Longing and The Word House traded worried glances. They knew that the Soul was someone of few words who, once she got going, lost herself to childish, idealistic enthusiasm. She would speak in crazy simplicities, like "Joy! Joy! Joy!" or just, "Like the Jedi sages say, let the Force be with you."

This time, though, her words left a trail of sorrow.

"Can't you just help me think of the plot?" Longing suggested.

"Plot schplot," The Word House bellowed. "Personally, kiddo, I don't care much for plots and, even less, for endings. Final solutions throw me into a panic."

"But, what about the formula *Post hoc, ergo propter hoc* . . . ?

"I see," said The Word House, as if she'd just read *The Structural Analysis of Stories*, "you need to organize experiences that never occurr, or that occurr only in your imagination. Don't you think it's enough to project a pathetic image, while saying real and horrible things?"

"More or less," Longing said. "More or less."

In her corner, The Soul had returned to normal and was chanting:

"The swallow wallows, for miles of hills, violoncello and swallow, in the gloaming the moon, at full gallop, swallowing, the swilling, swirling, swelling, squalling, squealing . . ."

"There are writers here who are infiltrators," shrieked a skinny kid with a green armband.

"And proud of it!" said Huidobro, making his first appearance.

He was late, but he arrived in style. He headed straight for The Soul, dressed as Cagliostro, ready for anything, reality, unreality, as if the revolution were intact, unresolved, invincible, far beyond the grip of history and the wolves of politics, beyond sorrow and fear, poverty and action, will and arrogance, a revolution made of everything that we are, full speed ahead in its carriage of living words, to the gallop of its horses made of wind, whose enormous hooves can make this very page tremble, as they are making it tremble right now . . .

VI.
Why Do You
Eulogize the
Rose, Oh Poets!

When Huidobro presented himself in the parlor on la calle Uruguay, he was the same as always, a soaring bird, flying almost as high as his poem. His first words were:

"You must understand that a poem is something yet to be. In other words, a poem is something that never is, but should be. Or, to be more precise, a poem is something that never has been and never can be."

"Please be so kind as to have a seat," said the monk without noticing that the parlor had no chairs.

"With whom do I have the pleasure of speaking?"

"Athanasius, at your service."

"Could you tell me anything else about yourself?

"Why not," replied the old man. "I'm an admirer of Ariosto and a disenchanted observer of the world. My reference book is *The Triumph of Fortune* by Sigismondo Fanti. My name, Athanasius, comes from Athanatos, which means Immortal."

He decided what to say arbitrarily, but Huidobro appeared delighted and immediately adopted a brotherly tone.

"What's the date today?"

"March 11, 1976."

"As I understand it," said Huidobro, "any excess of death or life (in this case, either way) conceals reality—is that so?"

"Yes," the monk conceded. "Only swallows rear their heads when it rains, and only to shake it from side to side. That's what I call having your eyes open to the impossible, and that's what the young woman and man, who often meet behind this very door right here, do. When their gazes cross, the miracle twitches like a monstrous spider."

"*Araignée du soir, espoir,*" whispered Huidobro, enthralled. "I'd like to give you a gift," he said briskly, pulling a tiny axolotl from his pocket.

"Thank you very much," the other replied, "I'll deliver it to my Museum as soon as the sun comes up, that is, if it ever agrees to rear its head again."

Huidobro permitted himself to smile.

"Of course the sun will rise. In fact, it's always coming out everywhere."

"Don't be so sure," advised the old man. "Outside, right at this very moment, as the two of us shoot the breeze, a man is walking stiff as an automaton up la avenida Santa Fe."

Huidobro waited for him to explain.

"Like night has come to his eyes to stay. And it's a sinister night, well aware of its place in history, which ignites all the sparks of hatred inside it."

Talking, Athanasius felt as if someone else were breathing inside him. It's difficult to explain something so simple. Somebody was breathing inside him, maybe someone with the same name as him, maybe someone just as easily disoriented, spinning, like him, around a lost axis.

"When that man makes it to this page," he whispered almost inaudibly, "there will be nothing left to do."

Huidobro remained cool.

"Is there any way I can help?"

The monk closed his eyes and saw that, in the *Nocturnal Annunciation* that Emma left on the table, a flower withered on the angel's cheek.

"The lily is dying," he said. "Now History will appear, suddenly, between two crows. Crows bring the dark. The young woman would like to inhabit her body but can't. She's motionless as a statue, ash-white, nearly transparent, between her bed and eternity."

"Yes," interrupted Huidobro, who seemed to understand, "I think I know her. She has taxidermy birds that peer from the corner of her mouth. The moon shimmers whenever she takes a step. Sad animals come and go, between her and the abyss, and vice versa. These are the degrees of the Great Secret. They cause me pain, her beautiful eyes of a victim."

"You intrigue me," said the old man after a time. "I'd like to ask you something. Do you think sorrow sometimes takes the form of pride?

"It's definitely possible. Love is a motionless arrow but every so often it follows its path from fear to fear, without stopping."

"So it is. Tragedy sowing its heavy silence..."

"Tell me about the guy who loves her," Huidobro pleaded.

"Oh, I'll never know how many deserts light up and go dark in that boy's head. Sometimes he seems furious, as if he wanted to escape words. Other times he ignores the fact that secrets, sometimes, leak out. It's like he can't stop affirming the impossible."

"And how old is he?"

"The age of sad men."

Huidobro thought that, sure, in life, certain truths come at a high price. He also thought that, that night, two grim nightingales would puncture the moon.

Neither spoke after that. The wait had begun.

A moment of silence, to observe the thrill of the unsaid.

No one has noticed, The Will thought, but I'm getting worried. Ever since I painted my nails and tossed out my favorite Ban-Lon cardigan, I've felt like a ditz. Am I getting dumber? What am I supposed to do? I rub my temples, but nothing happens. None of the higher-ups would call me *politically developed*. Not one would ever say, like the nerdy science major, *What I love most about your body is your brain.* I feel like I've lost my lost direction, efficiency, drive, ability to argue, ability not to see or touch or feel. It's my friends' fault. They're always saying "Don't be so stiff, stop acting like a kamikaze, you're *not* Wonder Woman." Maybe, to be fair, it's my own fault. No one is a harder worker than me. When I really apply myself, not God or Holy Mary can tear me away.

It went something like this: for no apparent reason, one day, I stopped reciting from memory Evita's *My Mission in Life*. I bought myself a vibrator, learned to play pool, spent hours shopping for underwear. Men started looking at me like I was emitting some kind of toxic perfume, one guy called me *Baby*, another told me *Andiamo a letto*, and poof, I started to feel sweet, positive, optimistic. I became the kind of girl with no past and no dreams (like film noir dolls). I even learned with the help of Alplax that, while passion might sting, it doesn't kill.

A real little gem!

"Very good, you get an A," I congratulated myself. "You've graduated from political education to sexual disorientation. Now you just need one more credit in fellatio."

I didn't find the proposition convincing. Wouldn't that be like taking up a kind of erotic diligence?

I'm lost, it's true, I need an aspirin.

I don't iron my shirts for meetings. I don't go out covered from head to toe. I even lost the habit of tucking my hair behind my ears, like The Wasp pointed out the other day.

In short, my head is splitting.

Recently I left the house with a suitcase full of condoms, and out of nowhere, I shouted: Trivial girls of the world, unite! For the object without a verb, subject, or predicate! For all we keep secret, especially from ourselves!

You could call it How to Become a *Queen*, and Die Trying.

Really, it's called, The Consequences of Explaining to the Body that Martial Law No Longer Prevails.

But what body am I talking about? The body is not the same thing as the body politic, or any body to which one might apply the adjective "stunning," or the body that is ignorant of itself, or the body of a text that, when written, receded into the distance, or the ethical, civic, athletic, religious, defeated, protesting, cynical, irritated, allegorical, or furious body, or the body as a nothing, dropping noiselessly into the river.

What am I saying? Who am I talking to? How long has it been since I set out for somewhere that no longer exists? And what is worse, *I* do not exist, much less my personal goals, if I can even call them that, these convulsive attacks of ambition that come on suddenly, who knows from where, and leave me on the Via della Penitenza with an inexplicable tremor in my chest?

I feel totally exhausted. And, to be honest, very alone.

What's the use of The Word House's irony, of Longing cluelessness, of the Soul's shyness, of Nobody's rules?

Could someone lend me a cardigan?

They'll tell me that I've fallen into delirium. Cotard's Syndrome! they'll say.

In its typical manifestation, Cotard wrote, the patient denies the existence of his own body. From that point, he denies the existence of his family, friends, time, space, and even of death. Delirium, in this way, is associated with notions of immortality. In its simplest formulation: I do not see myself = I do not see death = Death does not see me. Ergo, I cannot die.

Is it possible?

Maybe. There must be some explanation for the fact that I'm still *alive.*

Also, the secondary benefits are optimal. If I *cannot* die, that means that I can *suffer eternally.*

I feel compelled to socialize this finding.

Ladies and gentlemen, allow me just a moment of your attention. I hereby present to you, direct from the factory, with no middleman, a state-of-the-art delirium. Nine out of ten celebrities prefer it. This veritable utopia would cost you a fortune in the store, but I'm offering it to you today as a one-time promotional offer, not for ten, or for five, or even for three, but for the incredible price of ONE national peso. This delirium, yes, I'm with you, thanks, has a beautiful veneer of guilt, and it will never break (see how frantically I'm twisting and wrenching it and it's still intact?), it's simple to use, you only have to go out on the street in a nylon cardigan and cry to the four winds *I don't know you, I don't know you.*

I have no idea what I'm saying.

Luckily, The Unknown is still with me.

The Unknown is my realest possession. Sometimes we have long talks at night. I ask him, what does politics have to do with bitterness? Orphanhood with hatred? Hatred with creation? Do you think I'm smart, even though I paint my nails?

Then I tell him my nightmares. In one, the past is a ruined house. A woman greets me. She has a snake coiled around her neck, and she holds its head in her hand, right at eye-level. The snake gazes at her as if they were about to kiss. The woman inhales deeply, taking in its breath. And their breaths melt together until they are only a shadow, one long shadow that breathes in the world and, still in disbelief, I go back to naming things, and everything that I name is an absent intonation that my voice alone can carry, as The Soul would say, for the frivolous pleasure of swallows.

One morning, I thought: Utopianism is fanatical, and fanaticism is a *feeling*. "That's stupid," Nobody would have said, but I congratulated myself. If I have one idea, I can have others! I'm not stupid. *All* is not lost.

Where was I? Oh, right, swallows.

Who knows, maybe the swallows are all that exist.

Maybe they fly and alight on the wall, long since vanished, of the real house of the impossible, and that is, precisely, the *plot*: an indecipherable drawing, where childhood and the night, desire and dream, are suddenly synonymous with lost splendor. (I'll have to tell Longing about this.)

Maybe they are the ones who will speak for me when I finally lose myself completely to that person I've always forced myself to be. Then, I will put every little bone in a different box, and every box on a different shelf, every emotion under another name, and I'll leave, with painted nails, I'll frequent the cafés in Rome to discover the *emotional body*, as a friend of mine says.

The Unknown has been listening to me. He closes his eyes and waits. I don't really know what he's waiting for. For the delirium to pass. For my work ethic to kick back in. For me to get used to this new phase of political apathy, who knows.

"What else?" he asks.

I rummage a bit deeper, exactly in the place where I never was. I'd like to utter a phrase so beautiful it leaves me broken. I'd like to go to the other side of my eyes where, always, a sexual flower twirls. But terror holds me back, as if I were hypnotized by the abhorrent beauty of guillotines.

I'm just the instrument of a failed music.

A subversive woman, at the feet of her slyest questions.

"What is the date today?"
"March 11, 1976."
"Still?"

"Yeah. Yesterday was the suicide of Ulrike Meinhof, that German guerrilla woman who always smoked a pipe. Remember?"

"No... How come you're looking at me like that?"

"Last night I dreamed that I was looking at you from behind, Humboldt. You were an incredibly tall, furious figure, in a red silk *déshabillé*, burning down my house. What did I do wrong?"

"You forgot about the summer. What's the date today?"

"I already told you, March 11, 1976."

"What does the Weather Service say?"

"Partly cloudy, wind changing from east to west at 8 km per hour, relative humidity of 83%, rising temperatures . . . why are you asking? Am I ever going to see you again?"

"How could I possibly know? You'd be better off worrying about society."

"What do you mean by *society*?"

"Go look it up in the dictionary."

. . .

"Did you find it?"

"It's not there."

"Then just concentrate on what you lost today, when you traipsed into the future. And, while you're at it, stop conjuring me up, would you?"

"Do you think I'd move faster if I just tossed you aside?"

"I don't know, maybe at least you'd spare yourself the misery of writing."

"But, what about the kids we were going to be?"

"Don't talk nonsense."

"Just please tell me where you are when you're not with

me? Pleeease?"

"When are going to stop taking me for a wolf? Enjoy the free time to go out, read. Go to the movies, they're playing some really good films right now . . ."

"This is agony, I can't take it. I can't live without the thing I never really had, it used to be mine."

"Listen, we'd better call it a day, okay? Let me know when it's not March 11, 1976 anymore."

The music that corresponds with this scene is "Orfeo Fragmenter" by Bo Holten.

Dear Longing, little mermaid,

Looking at everything in depth, we still can't explain it. Who cares! So long as we avoid thinking of the hero's demise, his brush with nothingness, his tempest of tears. Behind every door, the wolves are still running loose, though they're tame. The friends of order shall one day see their monument.

Suddenly, a scream. Something arrives from far away— the night of the world? The explorer says: "Please, just don't let them take what I've already lost: all those clumsy rifles, that endless age of wonder that nestles, strong and sinister, into the arms of reality."

Don't give up, lady, your lover is just two steps away! Even if his lips are trembling. Look at him! Don't get sidetracked! Don't walk by wearing a blindfold! Everyone in the world is so lonely.

"It's over, for good," says an astronaut returning from the moon. Death really becomes him, especially in that exquisite white suit. Now night is falling. Will the dead rise again before the last human suicide? Who knows.

You may be wondering at this point, little mermaid, what you are reading, and I'll tell you the same thing I'd tell any reader: it's totally up to you. What happened to me, in my life, is irrelevant, or to put it another way, indescribable. What if I told you, for example, that I woke up at eight o'clock this morning, drank a coffee, and then ran away from myself? Words, as you know, have no public or private life. I always figured they were trains rushing off to settle some private disagreement and, in the process, to surrender to *life that's already been lived*, which is far more interesting than actually living. It's like always having to move on, to reach some abstraction, and to keep quiet about the things that really matter. You'll tell me that memories bring us closer to death, and I'll say yes, you have to watch your step. It's not easy to transgress a law, always heading for the next thing you've set your sights on, pretending that the unexpressed is the same as the inexpressible. Our violent instincts always shine through, and we lose our state of grace, whenever we try to avoid the hard work of pain. You just have to face things that don't have answers and trust that you'll always be able to say, at some point, with perfect nonchalance, *I don't know if what I see exists*, or even, *I don't know what it means*. Nothing is stranger, in the end, than reality. Were it not for the imagination, it would be completely unreal.

Oh, little friend, I know that ambiguity terrifies you, but it's my job to honor the truth, and for that, I need mystery. That's what I seek so relentlessly in my borrowed bits of prose: something that stays still, as in without a plot, aimless, no climax. You might just say, the present. What's the present if not a splinter, a presentiment that captures the blindness of the past and the inconsistency of the future? Even accounting for the fact that, of all the forms of unpredictability, only happiness is.

There's no room for error here. Things always make sense in retrospect, and that sense is always superfluous: in the end, there wasn't any sense at all. It's a terrifying conquest: when the curtain finally lifts, a voice announces, "Ladies and gentlemen, our only refuge is in the unknown."

As the author, I could still tack on a few confessions. I'm pretty skittish. I'm afraid of being who I am, and I'm afraid of fear changing me. Sometimes I can hardly stand it, like right now. I have nightmares about being swallowed up by things, myself included, so I live in a state of fixation somewhere between not being and its side effects. That fixation is a talent, but it has its downside. Sometimes I'm immune to the world, so it's hard to test my intuition that God is, among other things, our deepest misery. (I refuse to believe that God is just a golden dot that goes unseen.) So that's why I write, to draw myself into the horrible, which is the logical ancestor of the light. That's why I'm lost inside my own head, on an endless detour into emptiness, which fills me with unexpected strength.

Goodbye, dear little mermaid, I'll bid you farewell before I start pleading for help. All we can do is to wait, who knows what for.

Electronic kisses,

Your Emperor Très Noir.

P.S. I'll never wish you a happy Easter, I promise, even if it is March.

"And what about you, sweetie, how long have you been writing?"

"Ever since I started to believe in . . . tropical fish."

"Nice. And how is that working for you?"

Longing tried to look coolly observant. She thought in practical, scientific, literary, and esoteric terms. She was not, simply, foolish.

"Not too bad. At first, I got a little carried away in my wishful thinking. I thought that, if I read a million books, or if I studied the axioms of Gödel, Leibniz's indiscernibles, and Schopenhauer's fourfold root of the principle of sufficient reason, or if I could acquire, in a word, naïve genius, and if I really got the hang of failure, two failures per day, let's say, or at least once a month, or even once a semester, or if I could become..."

"Sounds like youthful promise," The Word House concluded.

Longing had no interest in a debate.

"Maybe, but if that were true, I would have gotten back everything I lost in the process. Obviously that didn't happen. For one, nothing turned up anywhere, and worse, I hadn't actually lost anything, I just didn't have it to begin with. That's when words started to enrage me. Why don't you become a reporter, a friend suggested. Give me a break, I said, I still have my principles. Plus, I won't write anything that isn't my writing, I'd rather face, like a great artist, the impossibility of existing. She wanted to turn me into a copy machine, can you believe that? As if words actually happened somewhere. I'll show them, I thought, and right then and there, I began to hate and write at the same time and, from time to time, something was born out of that maelstrom, unreal as the sea, for instance, or rather, like ships crossing time in the nebulous space of wonder."

"Sounds nice," The Word House appraised, with evident suspicion.

"I write, too," The Soul interjected in a tiny voice, "but, in my work, there isn't any hate. I'll always be what I am, and that's good enough for me."

"But you're notebook is totally blank, I saw it . . ." The Will reproached.

I really can't stand this girl, thought The Word House . . . Little Miss Bars- and-S stripes, a total control freak. . .

"That's not true," The Soul replied, flushed. "There's a swallow there, in all its forms: the one with visions recorded on its wings, the one that is Rome, before and after Rome, the one that's a bitter night when someone dies, and the one like the piece of the sky that shelters the absolute. Basically, dreams that people have long attributed to that flying body migrating between the season of necessity and the season of possibility."

Longing rid herself of that sentence as if it were a speck in her eye.

"If you like," she said, "I'll read you what I wrote today."

Without pausing for a second, she put on her glasses and began to read.

"*Ocaso*: Sunset.

Nearly a palindrome, whose initial circle is in phase with the final, signaling the uncertain crossing of the night that has yet to fall, in other words, destiny.

The explorer enters with his future gaze and says:

Is anyone there?

But no one answers. No one answers, because an answer would forbid something and, at sunset, unreality is the Queen of America.

The explorer feels vaguely uneasy, in other words, vaguely happy. He vows never to speak another word. Nor will he wonder what to do with his free time now that there are no limits whatsoever and, by extension, nothing to explore.

Silence. Silence in order to hear what silence says.

Any movement whatsoever involves risk. Any adventure on the part of the explorer with his suit of gold and his diadem of ghosts.

Sunset is a no man's land.

The sunset knows the explorer's vanity.

It is a question of life or life. Of finding the path of stones that lead back to nomadism.

The explorer surveys his instruments.

Then, he decides to obey.

The sky is his most faithful sensation. Sometimes, as they say, sunset will crash into the tree line, and something will become muddled, will change color and shape according to the direction of the wind, and the world will be set in motion, once again, to the delight of the heart and its prayers uttered in music and sand."

Everyone applauded on the spot. Everyone except Nobody, who was thinking 'this doesn't interest me, it's too out

of touch, it fails to take historical circumstances into account,'
stuff like that.

"Would you object," Athanasius asked, "to a brief
interview? I would like to archive it in my Museum."

"Not at all," Huidobro responded. "Shoot."

"What kind of novels do you prefer?"

"Detective novels."

"And why?"

"Number one, because memories got sick of hounding
me, and I was free to go and discover what is not *me* or *not me*;
number two, I'm crazy about math; number three, when blackness
prevails, images go wild and it's like seeing the giraffes at the zoo
all over again."

"Ah."

...

"What is writing, in your opinion?"

"To erase oneself."

"In what sense?"

"The most desperate."

"And what is poetry for?"

"For? Nothing. Apart from that, it's a house or a lecture
hall or a box that, like a *clavis universalis*, holds its own grammar,
the eternal image of the Beloved, the dialectic, the threat of losing
your life, Ovid's *Remedia Amoris*, holy days of penitence and,
above all, enigmas."

"How do you relate poetry, truth, and beauty?"

"A poem is beautiful because it sets up extraordinary situations that depend on the poem for their existence."

"What do you most dislike?"

"Crafts, gossip, reptiles, and Neruda, not necessarily in that order."

"What is your ultimate literary ambition?"

"To write a work that would not exist within literature."

"Poets who have influenced you?"

"Poetry begins in me."

"Tentative book titles?"

"Use of the Stars, First Night in Three Kisses, Dreamt with Winter in Mind."

"Do you have any regrets?"

"I could look out the window like someone searching for a lost word. I could claim that objects don't exist and, at the same time, that great celestial bodies spin in the sky and induce the human heartbeat. I could take issue with Kant, maintain that we are merely fuzzy disconnected impressions in a theater dreamed up by nobody. I could pray and think that devotion is everything and, even, collect my inspirations in volumes with ambiguous titles. But I have not written the poem of a broken homeland."

"What else do you hope to accomplish before you die?"

"To import nightingales to the Andes."

"What would you tell a young writer?"

"Embrace life, and let life be your song, not words."

"Is there anything you'd like to add?"

"Yes. In all my work, I prefer what simply *is*. It's the story of a very slow dance, so slow that the first part is like a question, the second is like an exclamation, and the third is like a sigh of longing. In short, I love simple plots. If it weren't for a tragedy announcing itself, the prima ballerina would seem to be in a dream: there she is, smack in the center of her obsession (if such a center existed), trying to conquer the heroic door to the world. In short: two pirouettes somewhere between wonder and doubt, a conclusion in a single swift impulse, and it's over. In a total of twenty seconds, you tear yourself away from childhood. You might call it: Inventing the Real."

"Try to act inconspicuous," interrupted The Unknown, referring to two cops who were walking into the café.

"IDs," said the dark one. "Stand up."

Everybody flashed their cards and hid their address books.

"Safe for now, kids," the dark one said, "but if I see you here again, I'll take you in for questioning."

When they left, Nobody wiped his forehead.

In the café, the TV was still on. The picture was no good, but the Leader's voice, by contrast, was unmistakable.

"I believe in almighty God, in the restorative power of the National Guard. Revolutionary war is not new, neither is guerilla warfare."

A student started passing out flyers. The book tucked under his arm was by Alvarez and Franco. The flyers read: *No conceding to the oppressor army. Free all political prisoners. Unity for all armed organizations. Victory or death in the name of Argentina.*

Long live Perón.

The Leader, escorted by his three poodles.

The masses chanted "Nation yes, colony no."

"It's all so confusing. Shouldn't we go over our slogans again?" suggested Longing.

"We've got our slogans down pat," said Nobody. "What we really need to review are our practices."

The Word House turned to face Longing.

"Remember *Bonanza?*"

"Yeah, totally. Who do you think is worse, Adalberto Krieger Vasena or the Mounted Police?"

"Stop being so clueless," said The Word House. "When was the last time you read the papers? Haven't you heard about the official end of innocence?"

"No. When did that happen?"

The Word House spoke in a tone of proclamation:

"Communiqué number . . . ."

Longing couldn't hide her panic.

"Why don't we let The Soul join the group?" she managed to say.

"No way," Nobody retorted, "She's a crazy vagrant, she's just going to muddle the issues. Not to mention, she only does what she wants to do, she'd make decisions off protocol..."

"I'm pro-alliances," said The Word House. "I say we bring her in, blindfolded, of course, for her own safety, but we should bring her in."

Outside you could hear Commissioner Villar's tanks. An icy cold seemed to be blowing straight from Rawson Prison.

"Spilled blood is nonnegotiable," said the kid with the flyers.

"I oppose the *continuism* of dictatorship," proclaimed The Unknown.

"Just between you and me, all that talk about a 'third position' between communism and imperialism," added The Word House, "is bullshit."

The Wasp thought it best to return to the source.

"If History is a limited number of decisive moments, and dead traditions can't be resurrected, I stand in favor of the happy use of liberty and against the danger of insect-ification . . . You wouldn't dare to say that he wasn't . . ." and he added after a pause, ". . . a real genius . . . an extraordinary mind . . ."

"And where does it say that?" Longing wanted to know.

"Obviously not in the Perón documentary," said The Word House.

"Did you know that the saying *Everything in its own good time* comes from Plato?" The Wasp insisted.

"So Plato invented organized community?" asked Longing.

"No, dummy, he was the inventor of Boyero sneakers."

"And who wrote *The Organized Death?*"

"Quit talking like a reactionary," Nobody ordered. He turned to glare at The Word House: "I am the Boss, you're my Subordinate, and if you keep talking like that, I'll have no choice but to punish you."

Free or alive, never a slave, The Word House thought. Ooh, look, I'm trembling!

Longing jumped in.

"Comrades," she said, "The Word House is part of the national middle class, which is not our worst enemy at this juncture. Foreign dependency is still our worst enemy. In the political arena," she continued, "it is crucial that we insert ourselves into different fronts, and in covering territory, as you know, the Word House is a natural leader."

How great you are, how worthy, the masses chanted.

The Wasp had begun studying the national Penal Code. His favorite chapters were "Crimes Against Life," "Crimes Against Freedom of Labor and Association," "Violation of Domicile," "Usurpation of Powers," and "Denial and Delay of Justice."

Someone on TV said:

"The Marxist guerrilla is extremely dangerous. We need order, an iron fist. If necessary, every last one of them will have to die in order to ensure the safety of the country."

"Who is that?" asked The Unknown.

"That's Disappearance calling," said the blind man with the stickers.

The kid with the flyers seemed not to have heard.

"Alberdi called violence the leavening agent of history. A nonliving wage is violence, too. Let's be perfectly clear, comrades," he said, "violence by the oppressed is not violence, it's justice."

Again, the unmistakable voice.

"I've ordered my Personal Delegate, we must be open to a generational renewal. To the violence coming down from above..."

You can feel it, feel it, the trap is set, chanted the Peronist Youth.

"What's this about?" the Leader asked one of his aids. "Don't they like the Peronist interpretation of history?"

"They want to steal your political heritage, General."

"As for the little punks who think they can have

Peronism without Perón, I'd like to inform them . . ."

"Perón gives the orders, we execute them," shouted the guys in green bracelets while hopping on one foot.

"Let's see how you deal with this," crooned the blind man with the stickers.

Pe-rón, Pe-rón, chanted the masses.

"I'm from the Young Catholic Students Organization," The Soul said timidly from her corner. "I have no *nom de guerre*. I don't like underground operations. I've never been a salaried activist, nor would I want to be."

The Soul seemed proud of her record. She was so absorbed in her speech, they couldn't stop her.

"And I hereby declare that I'm not interested in the motor of history, and also, I never went to bed with other groups, not the Mensheviks, or the radicals, or the People's Revolutionary Army, or the radicalized *tacuaras*."

"Hey, what if she's a far-right civil commando?" Nobody said.

The Soul wasn't sure what a civil commando was, but she wanted to sit at the table.

"Only group leaders at this table," said Nobody.

The Soul would have burst out crying if Black Fassano hadn't, at that very instant, walked over, shoved Nobody aside, and cleared her a place at the table.

The people, united, can never be defeated, chanted a communist in one corner of the café.

"Bolshie leftist shits," one of the green bracelets replied.

"It seems like," The Unknown said, "some sectors are super McCarthyite."

"I agree," said The Word House. "Just as many sons of

bitches in the Third World as in the First."

"It's a sad day for the country when the truest patriots are the ones subjected to brutal persecution. The time will come when there won't be enough lynching trees in Buenos Aires to administer the justice they have wanted for years."

"Who the fuck said that?" asked The Wasp.

"*Le Petit Monstre*," replied The Word House.

Nobody looked at her as if to say I'm going to blow a hole through your head.

Fight, fight, fight! chanted the masses. *The two-round ballot, they can shove it!*

Nobody took the reins.

"We won't let you down, General. You'll see, we'll bring you back home. With the unions leading the way, or with their heads in our hands."

"Shouldn't we explore some alternatives?" The Wasp proposed.

The Leader's voice lulled.

"I hear the most wonderful music, the language of the Argentine people."

Perón, Evita, la patria socialista, chanted the masses.

"There are outsiders in our midst, this is an organized threat, I've spent forty years in politics and I can spot an infiltrator when I see one."

"Booo!" shouted the groups from the middle of the country, "Stop busting our balls!" Everybody angrily turning back, leaving the plaza, "What do we do now?" Black Fassano said, "We need to give this flash mob a political direction." Nobody suggested a restricted meeting, but "we're in a march, man." Nobody stopped listening, refused to budge, his eyes darting, "the problem is we lack direction, we have to start immediately, work up a regimen, two hundred acts of harassment every day, any struggle is doomed without a leader," stuff like that.

"I wasn't wrong. The labor union stayed afloat for years, despite those screaming idiots!"

The green bracelets readied their batons.

"I propose we organize an escape plan," said The Unknown.

"From home to work and from work to home," the Leader continued.

"I'm confused," confessed The Soul. "I didn't grow up in a Peronist household, we never read *Radiolandia*, I never spoke slang like Tita Merello, I don't even like *mate*."

"Just like I said, they're trying to pass for Peronists, as if the t-shirt were all there was to it . . ." a green bracelet said.

"I can teach you the Twenty Truths," Longing offered. "1) for a Peronist, there is nothing better than another Peronist; 2) first Country, then the Movement, then men; 3) for a just, free, and sovereign Argentina; 4) children are the only privileged class; 5) people are our best resource; 6) when a Peronist begins to feel that he is more than what he is, he turns into an oligarch. I forget what what's next."

"Cut it out! It's just a question of balls," Nobody said, "and not forgetting that revolutionary struggle, driven by Peronism, is the only way."

Not Yankees, not Marxists, chanted the masses, *Pe-ro-nists.*

"I joined because of the stance on social justice," Longing said.

"I just joined for a job at the Student Union," confessed The Unknown.

"Well," said The Word House, "I have my objections. I hate systemic wars, the elitism in party hierarchies, sectarianism, bureaucratization, and all the scheming. I'm fascinated by the rear guard."

"This isn't a joke," Nobody said. "It's not easy to agree to sacrifice your life, your family, your loved ones, for an idea. War is the hardest thing there is: you're under heavy fire, you're with your fellow soldiers, there's the other guy, it's hell. I'm talking blood, shit, the smell of rot. You guys never give me any credit, but I know what I'm talking about. There is greatness in sacrifice. Man vindicates himself against fate. In moments like that, you feel like a god. Man throws his conviction into everything that's against it. Hard faces, threatened brotherhood, intense friendship, those are the real riches. You have to earn your death. It's about not ducking out or remaining faithful to the rules of combat. Yes, man is an end unto himself. War is his brush with his own slaughter."

Méfiez-vous des enfants sages, thought The Word House, who had read Sartre.

The masses chanted. *I'll give you, Beautiful Country, something that starts with a P.*

Suddenly it was silent. The sound of slogans dissipated.

"Fall in, everyone," said Death.

One activist lunged forward.

Nobody had seen him before, and everyone looked at him with surprise and, perhaps, a dash of envy. He was, at most, 22 years old, his eyes very black, his hair a little wavy, like Humboldt.

It was March 11, 1976.

Even the flies were motionless.

"I am very proud of having done what I did."

That was all he said. Death cocked the trigger.

That instant lasted an eternity.

The activist raised his arm, made a V, and said:

Onward to victory, General Perón!

VII.
In the Museum
of the World

Who told you that Rome is Rome, Humboldt?

Rome is the white night of swallows.

Roma: an anagram.

A city so beautiful that any enemy would be petrified upon approach.

I didn't know how to tell your story, Humboldt.

I left out many things, like the girl from Providence, how you sobbed that night in jail, and your helpless forbearance whenever you faced the enigma of your father.

Now it's eight o'clock. Eight is a fateful hour, especially if happens to be a rainy Sunday, and the river is blind and lazy, and there's that millennial coming and going from the window of the world to what can't be seen.

Not everyone, Humboldt, gets to choose how they die. Not everyone can proudly take the high road.

As for me, I have the right to prefer the image of you looking like a lost boat on a gorgeous stormy night.

Can you hear life arriving, how things take on the form of an obsessive song? (What do you call *that* feeling?)

Sometimes life comes to us like a spinning top, all wild colors. It comes, lets us inside its autumn, and then just as quickly turns its back on us, leaving us at the mercy of our own migratory impulses.

Swallows are slow to die.

Dreams, too.

I knew it because of my voice, the way it stood erect among the living ghosts.

One of those ghosts was you, Humboldt. I'll let you be, though. I'll stop cloaking you in sober heroism. I won't pick up your fallen name. I won't turn it into flag, and I won't sow discontent in anyone's chest. I'll erase the word "oppressed" from my vocabulary. I'll accept that it's over. Nobody will notice a thing. Nobody who might see me strolling down the Via del Corso with the studied dignity of a dedicated victim.

I can still say beautiful words.

Night of guilty eyes. Night that sees me. It is a night trailing from your body to nowhere. Here I go. The last music trickling out of me, *Hear, Mortals the horrible cry.*

Again, the announcer at the Trevi fountain. He is now prepared to bid farewell to the desperate poem. Ladies and gentlemen: *This is the sky falling.* Nothing remained standing. Not one fist raised to rebuke a blamable god. Only the swallows in their endless circular journey towards a deaf music. And barrels of quicklime. Songs killed by gunfire. *Coups de grâce.* And more fire, devouring everything.

Here is a beautiful speech proclaiming nothing.

You can fit many miracles in a single swallow.

A swallow is an act of faith.

As if to say everything will pass, something is searching

for us on the other end of the earth. Something with *broken chains.*

And here we have, again, though nobody beckoned it, hope, pernicious hope that injects itself like a venom into the body of reality.

All roads lead to Rome.

Prodigies are white nightmares.

Everything has yet to happen, repeats the sky, and I let you, Humboldt, and every one of the dreams that I embodied—the cities I lived in, the words I despised—dissolve into one vast, luminous nothing, like the one heralded by the angels in Emma's Annunciations, as sad and empty and outrageously beautiful as those *laurels that we didn't know how to win.*

"Who were we going to die for, Humboldt? I can't remember anything."

"Don't worry, it happens."

"What should I do?"

"Nothing, don't let them change your past, don't let them shut you out of History."

"What History?"

"The usual."

"Do you mean that the thing we wanted already came and went, only nobody saw it?"

"No."

"I don't understand. I don't understand anything lately: like, who were *our people,* why did Emma's neighbor dream about becoming a public accountant, what does the Fontana di Trevi have to do with the revolution."

"Did you look in my library?"

"Yes."

"Which books?"

"*Imperialism and Anguish, On War and Integral Command, The Historical Crossroads of Latin America, What Is to Be Done?, Proposal for a Description of a Reactionary Writer, Sex and Civilization, Examination of Conscience, Introduction to the Problem of the One-Party State, What is the National Ethos.*"

"And?"

"Nothing."

"That can't be, you have to read them more closely, look through the bibliographies, hurry, get lost, my head hurts."

"Is something bothering you?"

"No, I'm glad, we needed this whole debacle for you to find me."

"But I didn't find you. Nothing was on the platform. Nobody could tell me where life goes when nobody inhabits it anymore."

The music that corresponds to this scene is "Pas sur la neige," by Debussy.

Dear Longing, little mermaid,

Nothing has revealed itself in my borrowed bits of prose, apart from a sort of abstracted indolence. And in that indolence, in that nameless and featureless landscape, you were, like it or not, the third thief.

Have I followed the right path as a writer?

I must have. I always went in the direction of silence.

As for you, relax, and don't despair. Isn't it true that if something ends as soon as it begins, it lives forever?

Still, if I had to give you writerly advice, I would tell you: "Open your mind a little wider," "Follow through a bit more on your suspicions," "Even if the reader has a bib, you might not want to spoon-feed." In short: "Don't count on art saving anybody, least of all yourself (it won't)." And if you don't know how to start, how to continue, or how to finish, don't worry: content yourself with sadness. Who ever said that readers can't fly? That they never appreciate heartless sweethearts that gaze at us for two and a half sighs? That they don't aspire to get their thrills for one year and then die?

For my part, I am still far from my death. I have yet to embrace her, to receive her with open arms, like a neighbor: Hey, how's it going? Good thanks. How many shadows did you see today? None. How many fights? Tons. Where are you supposed to sleep? In a cold tower full of long-haired maidens.

This dialogue with my death never transpired. Not this or anything like it. Could I be so hypnotized by the notion of my own lifetime within Time, that I forget to make it through that hour of the night when language feels least like home?

Exaggeration, no question. My death isn't bitter, and I'm sure she'll find a way, when the time comes, to prepare me.

In the meantime, I study the swallows. There are so many things that justify migration.

That, and nothing else, is the mortality of the house. That, and nothing else, is the nameless enigma that we are, that we always will be.

I would like to add that I love all who are *alone in the world*.

Don't you think, little mermaid, that it's beautiful to be an orphan? An orphan is capable of anything: pretending, trembling because it isn't spring. Spring belongs, like everything that's incomplete, to happiness and no one. Poets are orphans. That's why they can replace what doesn't exist with what doesn't exist. Even then, they don't deprive themselves, not of kites, or conch shells, or cricket cages, which so often ornament their hateful libraries. The boudoir of fantasy, my friend, is truly marvelous.

And don't forget: there is no sadder violence than the word *island*. (I already wrote that somewhere.) There is a generous chaos, alien to all intentionality. There is, no doubt, the possibility of surrendering oneself to the desert and paying no mind to the wall of thoughts.

All that's left is an air raid fueled by future objections, like some utterly determined nonsense, between victory and its stakes.

I will write again very soon, more information to come on this bulletin.

Kisses, my distant countess.

Your Emperor Très Noir.

P.S. Today is the anniversary of my vocation, and I feel a little down. I'm still such a ways off from succinctly *not saying anything*!

Humboldt was thinking: Maybe this will get through to you. I can hardly believe my eyes when I see you in Rome parading through cafés, playing ping pong, taking squash lessons. I'm floored by your happiness. I'll tell you the same thing as always: you were a dark light. There's no other way to describe the winter you were. Come a little closer? What are you afraid of *exactly*? Your name on my lips, your pink dress with little flowers? Why did you hate me? It always went something like this: I come over, I say nothing, as if to say that I refuse to justify myself, I never learned how to tie my shoelaces, I'm a kid from Quilmes. We needed to live out, the two of us, the thing we dreamed. I saw it first, and you went blind, and the dream became mine. Yeah, I was spying on you, I'll feed your fantasy, I had to protect you, you were so delicate. You danced that evening. Slowly, smoothly, like naked pain, in your pink flowery dress, you're there, dancing. What time is it? None. You were dancing, and I illuminated you, that was my way of maintaining a *shred of dignity*, of holding to some non-negotiable principle. There are knots, I thought, in that heart, but I'm going to loosen them. Then like smothered fires in your hands, the remains of that nothingness: your poems. Your poems always sounded like blue litanies, full of rare sorrow, tireless wonder. I'll have to be content with that: *to watch* as you go, return, and leave again. Maybe love is fear, too. I'm going to die of you in that burnt light. I'm going to wait centuries for you to make a failure of me, for you to make me a pit where you can toss your solitude, your murkiness, your own body that you can't see. Fascinating, to see which forms can become formless.

Afterwords, events accelerated: the blind tempests of History. But ultimately, there was only the unbearable image of you, dancing. And of me, in my armor. Is that what it was like to love you? A hurricane that's none of my business? An ambition to lose everything? I could touch you right now, no one would see us, I could whisper something in your ear, who cares what happens to us, I left you, and you became me, painfully, I tore you open from the inside, open to yourself, so you might know yourself through me. It was a defeat in that way, in the extent to which it hurt us. Give me what I beg for at night, that pain I'll carry forever. It's not a lot and not a little. There will never be another reality. You'll be the joy that touched my life, and I'll be grateful. Losing you has been more than I can take. I don't know how to say it. I'll wait for that miracle for the rest of my life. Forgive me if I dream of you like that, like a child, hard as a pair of castanets, with eyes so light it startles me. If anything ever happens to me, yours will be the last face I carry. Don't forget it. Don't tell anyone. Don't write it down.

"Could somebody please explain our ideological conflict with Perón?" asked The Wasp.

"It's what you'd call armed arrogance," pontificated The Word House.

"Don't be a moron," said Nobody. "That's not the issue here, it's a question of reformist versus revolutionary politics."

"Are you saying that Perón isn't a revolutionary leader?"

"I'm saying that if we don't call the political situation what it is, if we lack a power strategy, if we fail to see that there are two competing classes and an ideological superstructure that serves the interests of imperial powers and their native lackeys, we won't have a strategy for tackling crisis in the regime, and Peronism will be co-opted."

"Try explaining that!" said The Word House.

"And The Unknown, where in the hell is he?" Longing asked.

"He's with a friend from Philosophy, trying to bring him in."

"Sounds like a waste of time," said The Wasp. "What difference will it make? He's been sweet-talking the dissidents for so long now, I'll bet you he'll be the next to leave."

"Anyone else want to leave? I got free tickets. . ." said The Word House.

"I'm sorry," said Longing, addressing Nobody in particular, "but how long until we finish this book?"

Longing, in a terrible state of longing, was trembling all over.

"Don't worry about that," The Will decreed, buttoning her Ban-Lon cardigan, which she recently started wearing again. "You'll write as much as you have to write, even if that means not sleeping, eating, making love, going to the movies, or sitting and having a coffee at the loveliest sidewalk café in the world on a summer afternoon."

"The army as an institution," the TV said, "is above men and is interchangeable with the Homeland."

The Wasp tried to lighten the mood. "Do you guys remember the song *Para el pueblo lo que es del pueblo*?"

"I can't stand Piero," said The Word House, "he's been singing the same damn song for years."

"Yeah," said Longing, "like Quindimil."

The Soul, who had just arrived, let her small voice be heard.

"Who's Quindimil?"

"The mayor of Lanús."

"During which administration?"

"All of them."

"Listen," The Wasp grew animated, "they just announced that, with Perón dead, the Montos have no more obligation to verticality."

"Fantastic!" exclaimed The Word House.

The Will was vehement.

"That only refers to verticality with respect to Perón. War demands sacrifice. A utopia is a utopia and, if you don't believe me, ask Tommaso Campanella. Anyone have an aspirin, by chance?"

What if I transfer to that cohort of swallows? thought The Soul.

She seemed willing to consider the option, but the TV stopped her in her tracks.

"The blood-soaked body of Representative Ortega Peña was discovered beside his automobile. Twenty-four spent cartridges were found."

"Ah, history," The Soul sighed, "why does it, like a fire, swallow everything, past and present, spirit and body, fear and hope, and then leave us behind with the word *childhood* in all its splendor, with white birds perched forever on the edge of the unattainable?"

In the dream, Humboldt, a series of bells sounded from the table of the tribunal, and the judge began to read, with a stern face, the long list of charges against me, for having, premeditatedly and maliciously, infringed, violated, contravened, without mitigating circumstances, the fundamental rights of fellow citizens, he said, in other words, for committing acts as defined by the rules established in the Penal Code of the Nation, while they led me to the bench and ordered me to respond to the question: Would I consider myself guilty or innocent. Oh Humboldt, I had to say something but no words came out, hard as I tried, my mouth dried up, and I couldn't look at anybody, until I was finally able to say, awkwardly, stammering, that before responding I would like to clarify one thing, I didn't believe that guilty and innocent had the same meaning for me and for them. I said something more or less like that, and then I heard the prosecutor shouting and ordering me to respond to the questions without resorting to linguistic trickery or meaningless wordplay. And then he commenced his lengthy accusation, armed group, he said, I had been a member of an armed group, I'd been a part of it, no matter in what capacity, adherent, mid-level, aspirant or official, the subversive apparatus, while he kept whipping out folders, and meanwhile, it isn't that I wanted to deny or much less repent for what I'd done, because yes, I said, I believe that this society needs to change, we're not here to judge ideas, thundered the prosecutor, but acts, specific acts that the law deems to be crimes and that have led the country into a horrific, deplorable bloodbath, or have you forgotten about the deaths caused by subversives such as yourself, what you have done is unspeakable, he repeated, and out of the corner of my eye I spotted the little notebook that El Bose had given me, and I took it, squeezed it in my hand, inside it was enclosed all the madness and happiness of that time, you

might as well forget, the prosecutor said, about trying to give a
social, political, or cultural justification for what you have done,
your direct or indirect responsibility for the crimes enumerated
in this case has been proven beyond a reasonable doubt,
your intention to incite chaos, to overthrow the fundamental
institutions of our democracy, such as family, education, work, no,
you were not revolutionaries, you were vandals, people motivated
by hate, and at best, you were immature and ill-prepared youth
indoctrinated by perverse minds in the breeding grounds of the
universities, schooled by a pedagogy of violence, incited to put
disgraceful principles into practice, but that in no way diminishes
how your bestial, delusional rampage has brought to grief
honest, innocent, Christian, working families, here they are, the
prosecutor said as he pointed to me and you, to El Bose, Emma,
and so many others who were now standing behind me, here
they are, he repeated, *they are the ones*, I thought, as he continued
with his speech, increasingly agitated, these crimes will not go
unpunished, he repeated, the country will never pardon the
perpetrators of this historical quagmire, stuff like that.

It's one thing to write towards death, Humboldt.

It's another thing *to write death*.

You risk keeping it alive forever in the folds of what
you say.

Now, for example, I have the sensation of postponing
something in order to linger endlessly in this cemetery of words.

Obviously, I survived. I never stopped to make sense of

the circumstances of my survival. I played dead for years. That's how it was. I went quiet, and something went quiet with me. The crowds, the march, the river.

Silence in Rome.

With the tapestry of a foreign city before me, with its ruins, mornings, infinite mirages, I could start another life. As if I'd suddenly regained, for some reason, my appetite for worldly beauty.

Occasionally, I'd feel the old, dull ache, whenever something from the *other* reality seeped into that earthly paradise.

Strategies. Cruelty. I did it. I ceased to be myself (but who was *myself?*).

And then I erected a house in the dry air of that emptiness.

I might have lived like that forever, wandering along the digressions of desire. But one afternoon Death walked up to me in a café. It was when El Bose handed me the notebook. He gave it to me so that I'd remember: dreams, self-defeat, epics large and small. All thrown together, on the tragic horizon of the century, with the counterfeit coin of ideology, verbal delirium, and that fear-driven arrogance that, I know now, becomes autistic and sometimes even bloody.

I need to breathe. I have to repeat to myself that, by saying this, I'm not betraying you, Humboldt. I'm not betraying *myself.* I'm not breaking a sacred pact. I'm not doing anything but facing my responsibility—hidden by the giant night of annihilation—for the spiritual, ethical, and political disasters that followed. I'm unmasking one of History's most heinous, opaque faces—with the dreadful feeling of having contributed to the apparition of that face.

Anyway, that evening at the Caffè della Pace, El Bose looked at me.

Under the Roman sky, in his open shirt, with his green eyes, he looked at me, and I could tell that he was tense, that a tension came from an otherness within himself. He looked at me as if he might find himself by looking at me, he might track down the same *longing* for freedom and justice that turned both of us onto politics in the first place, at another time that was also now and tomorrow and forever, and whether or not he found it, that idea shone and still shines with the fervor of a small flame that nothing, under any circumstances, could put out, not horror, or lies, not even infamous Death itself.

This time it wasn't him. I was the one to appear without announcing my arrival at the Collegio Romano where, according to his card, The Society of Jesus and The Museum of the World operated side by side. It was boiling in the evening sun, and I walked as if blind along Rome's golden streets, which revolve in a circle as if to suggest that eternity exists.

I found the doors to the Collegio open, and I inquired for him.

I arrived immediately at the Great Library where the old man, in a welter of papers and catalogues, was reading a book entitled *Sulla rappresentazione fortuita e casuale degli oggetti*.

"I never understood," I heard myself say without even greeting him, "why Emma painted Annunciations."

"Oh, it's you, Miss," Athanasius said, "I've been waiting for you for a long time . . ."

I didn't answer.

"You'll see," he said, noticing my lack of enthusiasm, "the Annunciation is an exchange of *caritas*. An orator, ambassador, *starry messenger* arrives and proclaims: 'Virgin, my lady, hurry and respond, proclaim the Word. And she rises, rushes forward, opens. It's as if she said: 'Give me what I need, not what I want.' At that moment, eternity enters time, immensity enters measure, the Creator enters the created, the unrepresentable enters representation, the unspeakable enters speech, the inexplicable enters words, glory enters confusion, just as in the preaching of Bernardino de Siena. Isn't that marvelous?"

He must have sensed my skepticism, so he tried another angle.

"Annunciation, dear friend, also suggests *enunciation*. There is effectively a greeting. And that greeting declares something—something like *Non est impossibile*. After that, it reaches Mary, who becomes house, throne, temple, the perfect city here below, which God can enter or, as Alberto Magno put it, stand inside and above at once."

"Ah."

The monk suddenly rose to his feet. Before I could ask where we were going, he hurried down the endless hallways and ordered me to follow. The Museum, I thought. We rushed on, and I tried to get a glimpse of The Hall of Maps, The Hall of Ancestors, The Hall of Toys, The Rooms of the Artists and The Happy Obsessions, The Hall of Remembrance, The Double Heart of the Unknown, The Hall of the Mythical Gods, and what grabbed my attention most of all, The Hall of Things that Touch the Absolute. I wouldn't call it dazzling. It was more like a monstrous, itemized repertory of human fantasies, an *alter mundus*, an odd spectacle of reality and fiction, where images are made and remade in places that don't exist, however compelling they are to behold.

"Maybe," the old man recapitulated as we entered the Room of the Annunciation, "they all amount to one Annunciation, which sprung from Emma's memory at the instant of her death."

The monk weighed his words as if they were stones.

Maybe, I thought, he too emerged from Emma's memory at the moment of her death. He, and his confiscated treasures.

"Doubtful," I said simply, "because that would negate chronological time, overriding History."

"Ah, my dear," he continued, "you still have a lot to learn. History is an endless burden, but the enigma of creation surpasses it. It's the duty of artists to become intimate with the universe."

"I don't understand," I had to admit.

"You'll see. What *is* cannot be won by human desire. It simply is or isn't, like Emma's blue, and you have to learn to perceive it in that split instant when it's not yet visible because it hasn't been touched by thought. Art would be, in that sense, the other side of History which, as you know, is no more than a way of thinking."

"And Emma knew that?"

"Emma, like all artists, far exceeded herself. If you don't believe me, have a look at that Annunciation. The only thing that really crystallizes is the halo, that vibrant fringe hovering over nothing . . . Look closely, and you'll see that the silhouettes seem almost diaphanous in their absence."

. . .

"To paint, Miss," he continued after a moment, "you
have to pass through many doors: the door of detachment,
dispossession, hardship, opposition or duality, the temptation
to seduce, the conflation of awe and desire . . . and most
importantly, exhaustion. Only someone utterly exhausted, like
Emma, can cross the threshold of her being, erase herself from
reality, and access the memory of the world, that shadow where
presence, eternally, explodes."

Athanasius quickly pointed to another Annunciation.

"Look here," he ordered. "In the blue of the trees in the
gated garden of love, Spring is erupting."

"Humboldt would have said that it's bourgeois to
think about spring," I let slip.

"And he would be wrong, of course," the monk said,
amused. "It doesn't take great wisdom to see how greed, misery,
and human dreams reside in the almonds of those eyes."

The monk gestured to a canvas that depicted, only, the
angel's eyes.

"Ancient times, and days yet to come, and every sort
of disaster, converge in that almond shape. If they didn't, it
would mean that the artist never shook off the shackles of fear,
that she didn't know how to free herself from her past, or how
to rise to meet it, because the future is just the past as seen
while flying. That flight is like a descent, from the senses, to the
senses, by which we shed the body of the mind. Only when we
embrace and accept that anguish, will fragility, our least evident
privilege, flourish."

. . .

"... If you'll allow me," he continued tenderly, "I don't believe that Emma ever caught the immense light of that paradox. She did, however, capture the fever of a beginning. In her determination to endlessly copy the Annunciation and reduce it to its essence, she turned up empty-handed. Emptiness granted her absence, which divested her of all tradition, all belonging, and led to the Book."

The monk's words seemed increasingly cryptic. In her paintings, Emma had omitted the missals. So what book was he talking about?

"The heart ... the heart," the old man said, divining yet again, my thought. "Every journey begins there, whether a journey across the world, or across worlds. When a heart opens, Time floods its inner walls. The present is that offering: joy that embarrasses us, beaming sunlight into our most intimate vertigo."

Something in that sentence made me lurch like an animal. My voice shook when I said, "Joy isn't the word I'd use to describe Emma's death."

"Oh, dear friend, any death, whatever form it takes, is a journey to grace. It is a fall, a letting go, an entrance into that powerful spiral that, in its total dispossession and excess, brings us to the bottom of ourselves. In death's incandescence, shadow has light, light has shadow. And duplicity of meaning is, perhaps, our highest paradise. But you have to earn it, you have to get there without stopping at the anecdotes that, supposedly, constitute life. Your friend Emma had a strong intuition for this. You might say that the very moment she set out in search of the color blue, paradise was already inside her. Her death, like mine, like yours, can't have the slightest importance when seen from this perspective, as you can imagine."

Suddenly I spotted, in a dark corner, a canvas covered with words.

"And that?"

"*That* is that night we've been referring to all this time, the night when Emma understood—or believed she understood—that desire, if partially satisfied, only reignites desire. That's what this Annunciation does: the Virgin takes the place of the stain, the angel becomes a slant gesture, and words are images again. The great Book of Reality is supplanted by the Book of Art, and the small sky of the soul gets ready to witness the terrible beauty of the divine. In other words, you are in the presence of memory falling through its own floor, a flaming arrow that lacks a set direction but, already trembling, is not willing to be rescued. Those words are birds lost in their own world—birds about to ask for the meaning of exile and migration."

"Swallows," I said startled.

"Who knows? What is certain is that your friend matured, became open to necessary work."

. . .

"Only in the end," the monk summarized, "is the paradox apparent. Light isn't light if it isn't fraught with shadows. In the shadows, you calculate time—or death, in other words—and also the ascent and descent of birds, the song that History sings to itself, the passion for shapes, wounds, crosses . . . Can I show you something else."

The monk stopped in front of a naked wall—with no pictures hanging—and I felt that, at that instant, the world flowed out of me and, at the same time, returned to me in its entirety.

Athanasius closed his eyes and said, as if praying:

"Now she covers herself with a blue shawl, she, only a girl / She covers herself in majesty because something comes to meet her, winged, a figure / It is the Angel, the Messenger / The air is on fire / What has always been missing arrives, and conspires to satisfy or injure / Over this nothingness Shadow descends, sovereign light / Glaring at her like a deserter, in the most extreme love / Immobile in her field of vision, in the glimmer of seasons / Exact, that desire's insolation / Something blooms on the bright border of the lived and unlived / Blue appears / Mystery made it through her work intact."

Rome doesn't exist, Humboldt.

At least not as the guidebooks promise, as a magic spell with healing powers.

I walk all over Rome only to end up cloistered in my room making another flyer—this time longer and more absurd— as if it were still March 11, 1976.

On the other side of the wall, beyond the *cortile*, the children have childhood. But which children? Which wall?

In my room there hangs a portrait under which it reads: *Humboldt, savant-citoyen du monde.* You're an empty profile, where a man offers a compass to a noble savage.

Have I mentioned that I lived for years in your company?

Beyond the wall, the children are playing marbles.

Where did my obsessions take me?

If you were here, Humboldt, you would want to leave.

You'd never have understood how the Romans live, what they think about, what they want. You would have said: I hate this fucking city.

It's true, Humboldt, the city is swarming with dark birds, with streets that never lead into any sort of caress.

If you only knew how *terribly* lost I am. I keep ahead, between your body and your body, living rock, an immense terrain, like a statue that can't quicken her own heart.

You will read nothing in his outrageous mixture of clarity and pain. Not even a sense of what you might have been.

It's called Lying.

I am, as they say, a bird of passage. A swallow that flew off, only to arrive at the place it never left. That's why it couldn't stop spewing lies, it had no access to the only real language, the one we speak when we don't speak.

You know, I have very little to offer you. A modern gesture, maybe, a dissolving panorama. A flash of a foreign city whose scenes fit, like theaters of cardboard and paper, one inside of the other, in fatal perspective. The city of the fear of the death of love. That is, the house of writing, house of suffering: a two-dimensional Guignol, totally fake.

I made it all up, without making up much, and you might say I haven't achieved that exception, that perfect dissonance, that happens when pure emotion—which I've never known—enters the soul's orbit and transforms itself into art.

Your image is a memento mori in my room in Rome. *Savant-citoyen du monde*. I'm about to give up, and I haven't even started. My characters are dead. All of them are dead, you heard me right, even me, especially me.

Then I wasn't resurrected? The whole party was

pointless?

The dark white night of defeat in Rome.

In Rome, Vespas ride alongside a blind yellow river, as if to calculate the time from the palaces to a sunset slower than fate.

I'm distracted. Like I was saying, the dark white night of indelible defeat. The whole history of shadow atop two sharply pointed letters, in cemeteries that do not exist. *Nullius Nomine*. Between reality up to here, and Reality up to *here*, what's the difference? Humboldt is Humboldt, like Rome was Rome. The children are still playing their game. The portrait in which you offer a compass to the noble savage. The military are still taking your body, the city where we were allegedly in love still stands, the eleventh of March 1976 drags on. The only difference is that you never existed, and that's my fault. You were left behind, gloomy, waiting for a miracle.

Maybe, you thought, if she'd only try a little harder, if she'd only hold on to the dream of History a little longer, then she'd really capture the thing that gleamed in our eyes as we talked about music graver than childhood and braver than the future.

Would that be faster? Could that shortcut zoom me to the white city of the urban night of the sweetest dream of the madness we held high like a lily announcing an era of light?

Unforgivable failure of this book.

I've said Rome as one says I'm sorry.

That's not enough.

You gave your life, and I cut a deal. There is no right word for that.

I'm tired, Humboldt. If you give me a compass, then maybe then I'd *see* death with all its lights, its empty niches. Thirty thousand. Then I would obliterate Rome once and for all, and I could lay a huge white sheet over everything we did and forgot, everything that I'm probably (who knows) killing right now, at this very moment, Humboldt—a huge white sheet that would purify everything.

It's a long road back, to the truth of things. I don't know which body I remember you in. I can't forgive you for your death, even if I made it up. I don't know how to move past that misunderstanding. I don't know how to find the version of you who smiled sometimes—not often, Humboldt—in our house with green walls in the city of the eternal night of a defeat that's always catching up with me, leaving me with nobody, laid open and vulnerable to my clumsiest battles, to the unbroken promise of dreaming, beyond Rome, Humboldt, beyond.

Acknowledgements

I want to thank Joyelle McSweeney and Johannes Goröansson for their trailblazing work at Action Books. I feel so fortunate for the space that they have cultivated for María Negroni's writing—not only for this lyric novel, but for my earlier translations of her poetry (*Mouth of Hell*) and essays on the Gothic (*Dark Museum*).

I am grateful to the National Endowment of the Arts for supporting this translation with a Literature Fellowship in 2012. Also, I want to thank my colleagues at Saint Vincent College for awarding me a Faculty Research Grant and, even more crucially, course release time to devote to this project.

While working on the manuscript, I benefited from the scholarship of Marguerite Feitlowitz on Argentina's Dirty War, particularly her book *A Lexicon of Terror: Argentina and the Legacies of Torture* (Oxford University Press, 1998). Also, I drew many insights from my father, Guillermo Higinio Gil Montero, who helped me to appreciate some of the persistent complexities of the time period and offered his valuable input on the translation.

Special thanks to Román Antopolsky, my collaborator in all things, for commenting on chapters of the manuscript and for offering me countless forms of encouragement, support, and inspiration. And I can't forget to thank the magnificent Annika Antopolsky for arriving with a loaf of bread under her arm at just the right moment.

Finally, I am deeply grateful to María Negroni—not only for her wisdom, patience, and guidance, but for the gift of her writing, which has altered my life and enriched me immeasurably.

María Negroni (Argentina) has a Ph.D. in Literature from Columbia University. Her books of poetry include: *Islandia, El viaje de la noche, Arte y Fuga, Andanza, La Boca del Infierno, Cantar la nada, Elegía Joseph Cornell, Interludio en Berlín, Exilium,* and *Archivo Dickinson.* Her essay collections include: *Ciudad Gótica, Museo Negro, El testigo lúcido, Galería Fantástica, Pequeño Mundo Ilustrado* and *El arte del error.* She has published two novels, *El sueño de Ursula* and *La Anunciación,* and two collaborative books: *Buenos Aires Tour* and *Cartas Extraordinarias.*

She has been awarded grants from the Guggenheim, Rockefeller Foundation, Fundación Octavio Paz, New York Foundation for the Arts, Civitella Ranieri and American Academy of Poets. She has won a PEN American Center prize, Premio Internacional de Ensayo Siglo XXI and Premio Konex Platino. Her work has been translated into English, French, Italian, Portuguese and Swedish.

She is currently the director of the MFA in Creative Writing at the Universidad Nacional de Tres de Febrero in Buenos Aires.

Michelle Gil-Montero has several book translations, including most recently, *This Blue Novel* by Valerie Mejer Caso (Action Books). Her work has been supported by the NEA, Howard Foundation, Pen/HEIM, and Fulbright. She has one chapbook of poems, *Attached Houses* (Brooklyn Arts Press). She is Associate Professor of English and director of the Literary Translation Minor at Saint Vincent College.